7/
19/8

The Cost of Living Like This

THE·COST OF·LIVING LIKE·THIS

JAMES KENNAWAY

Introduction by
Frederic Raphael

MAINSTREAM

This edition published by
MAINSTREAM PUBLISHING COMPANY (EDINBURGH) LTI
28 Barony Street
Edinburgh EH3 6NY

The publisher gratefully acknowledges the financial assistance of
the Scottish Arts Council in the publication of this volume.

ISBN 0 906391 08 3

Printed in Great Britain by
Billing & Sons Limited
Guildford, London and Worcester

For John Browne

Introduction

by

Frederic Raphael

I remember James at the top of some stairs in a tall house in Pont Street. A wedding was being prepared. There were people we both knew, people we did not: each other. He had published *Tunes of Glory* in the same week as my own first, petty book. We were reviewed in the same column in *The Sunday Times*, he at the top, I at the bottom: there was resented justice in the placing. He had been at Oxford with the bride, I at Cambridge with the groom. He was my evident senior and his energy (the stairhead shook on his arrival) promised that there was more where that came from. He had been a soldier, of course, and he was a Scot, conscious of blood (it showed in his cheeks). We met in that busy room – the women hurrying and laughing, save for the plain one, who would never marry, or divorce – as if on more serious business than we ever managed to transact, friendship perhaps. Friends of friends we remained, with the emulous fraternity of authorship bond and obstacle between us.

Tunes of Glory was a warning trumpet to me: there were serious things to do. I was somewhat mortified (soldiering being his subject and I a civilian) by the early knowledge he showed of terrible things, not least defeat. He was a conqueror in his style, virile with the right of entry he revealed as he burst into that loft, yet he knew the nuances of defeat, rejection, pain. He was sensitive to women and could inhabit them, if always with a touch of vanity. (How they wanted their men, his characters, the two in *The Cost of Living Like This* being manifest instances!) He never boasted of success, was prompt to settle to writing as a *métier*, hence the screenwriting, but never at the price of callousness or calculation. He made success the opportunity to touch life's bruises, if only in salute, the officer's acknowledgement of other ranks. He had the military style, but he knew the nakedness beneath every variety of uniform (even the referee's, who holds the ring – see the character of "Mozart" here).

He was a provincial, I suppose, but London could not surprise him. He rode out its ambushes and scouted its dead ground, outflanked its coteries and became, quite soon, a seasoned campaigner. There is no strain in analogising writers and soldiers (though no medals for courage should be given the former). The clipped style goes back to Caesar, though there was little Gallic in James' wars, unless it was the prevalence of the tripartite plot (*Gallia tota*, after all), the adulterous triangle; there is, of course, something conveniently aesthetic in the form, since it breaks up the endless duologues, as James himself points out, so typical of marriage. But he refused to make mere literature out of living experience (not his necessarily, but his time's). He forced life into the page; savour his dialogue and you will feel the barbs still in it, the poison no less than the poise. Watch his characters and you would swear that they were struggling to get off the page; they go down fighting, like Julian in this, his last novel.

He was without pretentiousness, yet he grappled with the big subject, life, and deferred to no other man's vision of it. He was not experimental, but he was novel. He was a professional and appeared to relish the hard shameless test of the movies, and the money, I daresay, that bought independence from griping London. He saw the terrible things in domesticity, yet celebrated marriage even when he was honest about it. He was a writer of the Fifties and Sixties, the couple his husbanded territory. He came of a time when people worked at their marriages and felt failures when they failed.

His work speaks for itself. Another writer must honour it for its autonomy. One may quibble with his way of doing things; one cannot lift it. He is always curt and never uses lofty phrases or erudite allusions. He profited from his cinematic experience, I suspect, to abbreviate as much as possible. There is a dire form in the movie-writer's repertoire called the "treatment". This is a story, told usually in the historic present tense, with some dialogue, which gives a fairly short summary of a film which may or may not come to be written (depending, usually, on whether a commission follows). It is a humiliation, very often, to be asked to produce such a narrative, but most of us have done it, when needs must. James elevated this sullen form into an aesthetic. He "collapsed" incidents, inter-cut them, and gave his characters a short time in which to make their claims on our attention. He took no nonsense from himself, or them. There is no whimsy in this view of the novelist's performance: our characters are like casual guests, who must make their mark or be gone (if only one could be as abrupt with people!). Kennaway's art is short with artfulness, but only to conceal it, as the magician rolls up his straightforward sleeves the better to prove how honestly he will hoodwink us. The reader may, if he can remain aloof (which I doubt), amuse himself by trying to make cuts in *The Cost of Living Like This*. I doubt if it is possible to excise more than, say, a dozen lines.

James Kennaway and I did not, I think, meet more than three or four times. Our friends married and did not invite us together; we never invited each other. They were in Italy; we were in Spain. He and I published at separate times thenceforth, never reviewed each other (luckily), never wrote. Until, in a certain season, after a success, I had a misfortune. A film on which I had lavished much effort (and love, of a kind) was savagely received by the London critics. I published a novel at much the same time. It was equally gored. I fell heavily, though not, I think, in public (my friends, who hurried to say that I had had *another* bad notice, perhaps could not imagine how much I cared, or didn't care). It was then that I received a letter from James. He promised me that my work was well regarded by more of my fellow-writers than I might think and he advised me, in words I wish I could always honour, not to "flail away", but to keep on writing, which was the best revenge. I have seldom been done such an uncalled for or necessary kindness. I responded with a certain stiff gratitude (ah these British habits!) and wished, at my great age of thirty-six, that we "might have been friends". (I am not sure what I thought stood in the way.)

We were about to leave on a long trip to South America,

cure and purge. We spent some time in Argentina and then in Peru and Jamaica, cut off, thank God. We returned in the cold January of 1969. I was soon speaking to a producer, who wanted me to write a script for him, and being too busy to accept the job, I proposed James Kennaway. "He's dead," the man said. I could hardly believe that someone with so vital a charge in him could really be gone: "James Kennaway? *Dead*?" I regret him often, as I do my own stupidity in being so stand-offish when I had the chance to know him. It would be amiable to say that his work still speaks for him, but though it certainly does, it is not enough, not nearly. I am conscious, reading *The Cost of Living Like This* once more, how brief is a writer's career, how brief is life itself, and there is something painfully ironic in this last book, about a man fighting against the dying of the light, having been written as the bracket was closing on Kennaway, James (1928–1968). He should have had longer; we should have had him longer.

Frederic Raphael.

Chapter One

T HEY were painting the gothic corridors of the railway hotel when the economist arrived. It was about six o'clock in the evening, early in May, which is no time to die, and it had been raining heavily. His grey greatcoat was wet and his hair was soaked. The economist never wore a hat.

There weren't many people in the hotel. The painters had shifted some settees and chairs away from the walls: they lay about the lobby as if they'd been washed up by the tide. The economist just managed to reach one of these. He tried to keep sitting upright. An old and officious porter stared at him glassily believing him not merely to be drunk but to be *a* drunk.

Fair enough: the economist could have been mistaken for a dipsomaniac. His greatcoat had been cut for him some years before. His shirt was silk, but it was frayed at the collar and cuffs. His shoes were wet and muddy as if he had been walking for hours; forever. One sock was navy blue, the other was black. His hair was long and thick and colourless and his skin was the same tone as the cream on the top of a bottle of milk. Not unlike a dipso, to be sure. And falling sideways, the economist thought, Lord, if it were as simple as that.

The nurses call it jungle-juice, the bright little nurses from Wanky, Worcester and Wanganui: the ones who can bear the pain. They say it's gin and honey, what could be nicer than that. They don't mention the heroin, morphine and cocaine which also go into jungle-juice. And if you listen to the doctors on the television programmes they will tell you that it is quite unnecessary, these days, for patients to suffer. "We have the knowledge and the drugs," they say. But the economist, like most other people we know, had developed an "exceptional" resistance to the drugs.

Instead of half a grain of morphia every four hours he was taking two every two hours, also paraldehyde, and it wasn't yet the end for him. In the hospital, they told his wife Christabel that they were doing all that they could for him. When he came home, the local doctor said that if he continued to prescribe that weight of drugs there would be a Home Office enquiry.

The economist woke from an eternity, a vast and velvet gothic womb, twenty seconds later, when the porter shook his shoulders and said "We're not having this, you know."

The economist could remember the strange purple colour of the cloud above the bright green grass and trees in Hyde Park. He had never seen such a strangely beautiful colour, nor brighter green. And white buildings, below.

The porter said "You can't settle down here, oh no you can't."

The economist was not a big man, but neither was he old. The weight of the drugs alone prevented him from smashing the porter in the face; from splattering his nose as if it were a fat and bloody insect on a wall. The economist's eyes were pale but there were rings round his pupils which looked almost black.

"Don't you look at me like that," the porter said jumpily. He was like a groom afraid of the evil in a horse's eye.

The economist struggled to his feet. The pain was very low tonight and it was getting sharper. Sharper. Christ, like a cramp of the bowels and for a moment it grabbed him, the bloody crab grabbed him in iron claws making it impossible now for him to walk. He could no longer push one foot in front of the other.

The porter said rudely and defensively "You're drunk."

Very quietly the economist replied "No, friend, I'm not drunk."

The painters were looking down from their platform but they didn't say anything, didn't reckon to get involved.

The economist leant back on the arm of a chair. He should have been shivering with cold after his soaking in the cool summer rain but he was breaking out in a sweat. It gleamed on his yellow brow. He started to struggle out of his heavy wet coat and something about him, some strange adventurous authority, made the head porter, who was a younger man, come across and help him. For a second there was an air of mystery, like the beginning of a ghost story. When another traveller came through the swing doors there was a little rush of wind.

The economist had bought five panatellas, long, thin, black cigars. He lit one with some difficulty. Then quite suddenly he walked straight along the corridor to the bar, the big travellers' cocktail bar. He fumbled for a stool and sat down.

The barman had already put a Cutty Sark over the ice. He was the best barman in London.

"How are we, sir."

It wasn't a question. That barman never pried. "And Madam?"

The barman didn't mean his wife Christabel; didn't even know he had a wife. The barman referred to the girl called Sally who so often met him here.

The economist asked for a quarter of a lemon and sucked at it, almost ravenously, sinking his teeth into the rind. Then he took a sip at the whisky. He sat trying to recover his breath.

He wasn't much more than thirty-five. In his profession, if it's a profession (and he spent half his time proving to governments and bankers that it was only a specialized guessing game) he was a "name", but not to anybody else. His christian name was Julian.

He said "I'm seeing her tonight."

"She coming in, sir?"

The economist shook his head and faintly smiled. He thought about the barman, you're a great London barman; about the hotel, you're a monstrous, marvellous Victorian London hotel which I feared I'd never reach across the wastes of pain.

Then suddenly he felt very hot about the face. The barman had provided him with an evening paper in which the Chancellor said that devaluation was unthinkable. Some girl was getting a part in a film. There was a cartoon about Jews and Arabs. The economist dared not let his mind dwell upon the people in the streets or the colour of the park trees or the reassurance of the barman who did not pry. And it passed through his mind: I am not tired of London, I am not tired of life. How can we do it, how can we be put on the rack week after week and want only to survive?

This barman does not know how much I like him, the economist thought, not only because he knows me with Sally Cohen, but because he is living and working, and not asking questions, in London. He pours me out another Cutty Sark.

The economist knew that if he went to the cloakroom he'd never get out on his feet. He'd lie down there with his cheek against the tiles on the floor.

"Yes, I'm seeing her tonight." Seeing Miss Sally Cohen in Half Moon Lane in Herne Hill, London, S.E.24 tonight.

The barman leant forward and said, jokingly, in a low voice, "Any time you want to give her up, sir, tell her how I'd like the option."

"I'm sure she'd give it you."

"She's got those black eyes, has she not."

The economist wanted to give the barman forty pounds. He was carrying more than that. He wanted to shake the banknotes over the bar and let them drop amongst the tonics and beers like leaves. He put down a pound only and shoved the rest back in some pocket. The pain had been worse than this, a lot worse.

"Thank you, sir," the barman said. "Give her my love."

"Oh yes."

And Lord, the economist thought, the games we play, even when we're sick like this. Perhaps *because* we're sick like this.

The wicked games, the weapons we use to destroy others with ourselves: there is no measuring the lengths to which we go in order to avoid the loneliness of death.

They brought a taxi for him, right to the hotel door. He would not let the head porter take his arm. He found the steps a little difficult: they seemed to vary in height. But in the cab, the seat was comfortable. Sitting at a certain awkward angle in the corner he could, for seconds at a stretch, get out of pain, and could anticipate the pleasure of Sally's small, broad face; the black eyes; pink mouth. Lord, the games.

No one really guesses the games which are special to the dying. No one would believe them, if they were told. No one has mastered them, except the dead.

It is the doctors who serve first. They say—"Call it cancer, call it catarrh. What's in a name, we merely have to find out if it's malignant and if so, we not only chop it out but give you a spot of treatment."

"I've heard of deep-ray treatment."

"Deep-ray's just a name."

"And is the growth malignant?"

"Well, that's what we're going to have to find out."

"And if it is, will you tell me?"

"What d'you mean?"

"Will you tell me if I have cancer?"

"Well, of course we will."

"You, Doctor. You personally."

"Why the hell shouldn't I, old man? That's by no means the end of the story."

No, it's not: too right, it isn't.

Another cigar at the most, the economist thought as the taxi raced down the wet streets. They have a strange new one-way system in Victoria and Pimlico. Another cigar, no more. Isn't it extraordinary to think that men take alcohol and drugs when they are not in pain? Yet, Lord, how I would smoke, if I could again reach the end of a cigar. At least we can light up. In a moment we will be where we said we would be again, only this time in reality, not in a poisoned dream: South of the river. Londoner's London. The London of all the Sally Cohens.

The economist did not like doctors. Some invalids seemed to trust them but doctors and Christians shared a naïvety which the economist translated as conceit. He did not like men who pretended the world was something different from what it is. "From what it is" sounded like a Sally phrase.

South of the river, where they eat fried food... Soon he'd smell again the house divided into separate rooms and flats. All the doors had Yale locks. Sally was on the ground floor, which was divided and shared, front and back. And as they sat there, the front door would bang...

8

"Sid?" Sally would guess. "Or Simon." Then the footsteps would cross the hall ... Jump upstairs two at a time. "That's Sid. Hey." She always said "Hey". "Hey, did I tell you we've got a new girl in 7A? She's pretty. Full, you know, like my sister Shelley. Not really fat. But she's not my type, this girl. She's big-headed, I think ..."

Sally in purple corduroy slacks that weren't very slack and some light childish, natural, maybe Shetland jersey, surrounded by LPs: Johnny Mathis, Beatles, even Cliff Richard ("Don't you think I look like him? Like his sister, I mean?") ... Dead flowers in a vase, empty bottles of coke on and behind the rented TV ... Empty packets of Stuyvesant cigarettes ... "You wouldn't have a ciggie, would you?"

And "We're not doing it here," she'd say, stepping over the debris, "by the way."

Sally in Sally's limbo, completely unworried, with everything up there, ahead. "Jacky's getting married July, didn't I tell you, I'll be on the shelf. At nineteen. Well, in my nineteenth year."

For instance, when other people went into a surgery, the economist wondered, did they not also secretly hate the man in the white coat? Didn't they too feel sickened by the complacency of his common sense? The economist couldn't abide it when the Sister and nurses puffed up the pillows, saying "Doctor's coming round." He used to offer the nurses cigarettes when the doctor was in the room.

"Well, old chap, how are we feeling today?"

"Stiff."

"Stiff?" This doctor was so superior that he called himself Mr and wielded a knife. He yachted. Everybody knew he was a sailor. The nurses prompted the patients, who then had to pretend to be interested in some transatlantic sailing spree. The Mr Doctor, lean-jawed, clear-eyed, self-navigating six-footer, then said a few spicy words about winds that prevailed in the Azores.

"I should think you do feel stiff, old man, after what we did to you yesterday. We had you sliced open like a kipper."

Thanks, skipper.

The economist could only take short breaths during this interview. Doctors combine an air of masculinity with an impression of virginity. They look as though they change in changing-rooms and never drop their eyes. The economist did not like doctors. He preferred mini-cab drivers really, they being the other idiots to whom we so frequently trust our lives.

The doctor had asked "Are you the kind of patient we tell the truth to, or don't we go into all that?"

It should have been obvious that it was a dummy pass; that no doctor was going to say "Terminal cancer, so forget it, son." But in the presence of doctors, playing on their ground, shackled and winded, we have no return.

"It's the lung. The right-hand side," the surgeon said.

Who cares which side? As if we hadn't all known it was the lung for several months. Who's breathing, after all?

"Quite certainly," said this surgeon proudly, as if he'd made a discovery overlooked by two specialists, one family doctor, and an X-ray unit. "Yes. The right-hand side. Your right, that is."

The taxi proceeded through the wet streets of Brixton. The economist took out his black handkerchief and like an infant after too rich a meal he was effortlessly but only slightly sick: just the whisky back again.

Sometimes the pain was higher in the back, almost between the shoulder blades but when it was there it wasn't so bad. They said that might have to do with the deep-ray treatment. Or possibly it was merely muscular distortion after the long period in bed. Or, like the bad pains below, some reaction to the drugs. They had answers which the economist accepted. But acceptance is not quite belief. Acceptance is a blind drawn down neatly between patient and the blazing truth. The chinks of light show only in the dark and lonely hours before dawn.

The economist stared out at the rain and at London. Big black men kept running across the shiny streets and others sheltered by the doors of empty cinemas. The economist threw out his cigar. The black men seemed to favour skinny white women, maybe with buck teeth.

Long ago, a year ago, after the lung operation the economist had left Oxford to do a spell of work for the Government. That was how he met Sally Cohen. She worked downstairs in the miserable warren of the building in which he was paid to think. Downing Street only holds the big swells in the Cabinet Office. Junior thinkers are to be found in boxes as far afield as Pimlico.

Julian was housed in an office from which he could watch the garden at Buckingham Palace, when he wasn't counting out some deficit. He wasn't accustomed to club luncheons. It was the Duke of Edinburgh's helicopter which woke him in the afternoons. Woke him pleasantly, because Sally Cohen, who was the most junior kind of junior, used to rush into his office and lean out of the

window and wave and yell and shout "Any time, old
Duke." She was the only individual Julian ever met who
had a completely rational objection to the Monarch; she
envied her, straight.

Sally wore her pants outside her tights, and they showed
when she leant out of the window to yell.

"They're blue, today," Julian said, one day, and it only
took her about half a second to catch on.

"No, they're not," she said. Then looked. "So they are.
You're married, aren't you?"

The economist was never fast on his cues.

"Yes, Sally. I am. With two children."

"Girls or boys?"

"Boys."

She sounded as if she had lost interest as she echoed
"Boys, that's nice."

Nobody in the whole building (which still housed some
of the sad remains of the Air Ministry) called Sally anything but Sally. Nobody knew her exact job, though she
constantly outlined its limits. "I'm not in the typing pool,
and I don't care how much Stan asks and fusses I'm not
going down the mine any more"—the mine being a department mysteriously labelled "Accounts".

"Is it true how you were ill?" she asked.

"Six month ago."

"In hospital?"

"Yes."

"I've had an operation, beg pardon."

But at the door she turned back again. She looked quite
serious.

"What grade are you?" she asked.

"I'm not. I'm on a year's salary."

"Oooh. Is it big, don't tell me."

"You can find out."

Then one day he said "I make enough to buy you a drink."

She frowned at that.

She said "Cynthia fancies you."

"Who's Cynthia?"

"You know Cyn-thea," she said, "our Cambridge graduate," and pronounced it with a long, long "a": *graad-you-ate*. She went on again "You know, one that works in Central Filing. One that gets the books for you."

"Miss Bell."

"You just have to ring 218. I can tell you. Not that she's said anything. No, no, not Cynthia . . . Honestly, she's got you very bad. I should know. I'm meant to be her assistant." Then she added "I think."

He said "It wasn't Cynthia that I noticed when I went into that office."

Very gently, "Oh wasn't it? I don't drink."

Julian said "How old are you?"

"Seventeen, nearly eighteen."

"I'd only corrupt you."

She admitted, long after, that she didn't literally understand the meaning of the word "corrupt". She said at the time "Perhaps I only want to be corrupted."

But then the Duke flew in, so she rushed to the window. She was still shouting "Now, now, me, me" and other merry, loyal rejoinders when one of Julian's colleagues entered the room: the Permanent Secretary.

Sally was sent down the mine and spent her days punching cards. She read bad novels very slowly and dreamed of winning the county swimming championships. This wasn't altogether a wild dream. She was in the class. She said she could do it if she could only stop smoking. But if she stopped smoking she bit her nails.

So Julian saw less of her, but he knew where she worked and he passed her, sometimes, at lunchtime. She sat in the courtyard, on the wall, eating sandwiches, talking too much to the other juniors, male and female.

He'd ask her "How's the Duke?"

"Ooooh," she'd cry, in pain.

Really, at that time, he saw her exactly for what she was, which was a sweet cockney girl too young even for a Pepysian affair. Meantime he laboured on, upstairs, trying to calculate the correct measure of devaluation in the light of probable European repercussions. He had thought that devaluation had already been decided upon. He was only one of many who recommended it at the very beginning, when the Government first took office. But this did not turn out to be the case. The Chancellor decided to stick with the pound. And the consequence? Not only the total collapse of confidence in sterling, but also, some spare time for Julian. Worse than spare time: a continuing feeling of effort wasted.

Ponces should have noses which potential clients can confidently believe to have been in worse places than their own. Just such a nose had Jack-the-caretaker who was not much taller than Sally. He had a bald head, bandy legs and a Scots accent.

"Here a wee."

"Huh?"

She was leaving the building, on the dot, as usual, her towel and bathing suit wrapped neatly under her arm.

She was swimming in a match at Holborn Baths, that evening.

"Here."

She said "Ouch. What have I done now?" And he beckoned to her to come out of the corridor into his horrid little glass box.

"I've a message for you."

"For me? You're joking?" At first she seemed excited. "Why didn't you send it downstairs?"

"From an admirer." Jack winked.

She frowned. She said "Oh I thought it might be from the A.S.A."

He didn't recognize the initials.

"Amateur Swimming Association," she enlightened him. "'Dear Miss Cohen, you have been chosen to go to Hampstead and thereafter to Stockholm as first reserve woman's free-style individual and relay for England.'" Then taking the envelope from Jack, she added "Don't mind me. Every stranger comes up to me, I hope that. I'm a swimming bug or buff or whatever it is."

Jack said "I was an athlete myself." He kept nodding and bobbing at the senior people leaving the building, behind Sally. She opened the letter slowly, saying "I suppose this is some kind of horrible hoax." Her "Rs" were never too clear, yet she didn't exactly say "howwible".

She read the letter, apparently with difficulty; began to read it again.

She asked vaguely "Can you swim, Jack?"

"I can't swim."

"Why ever not?"

"In my day the schools never took you to the Lidos, so I never learnt."

"How old is he?" she suddenly asked. She meant
Julian.

Jack thought "Thirty-eight."

"Chrr-wist," she said, "he's not that?"

"I should think so."

"No. Thirty-seven at most."

Jack laughed. "Is that so very different?" The double
reaction was typical, somehow, of Sally: the shock of
thirty-eight, followed almost instantaneously by an ad-
justment to the situation.

Jack was going on, "Some is older than that. And still,
on the game. We'd a Life Peer I hauled out of a wee flat
onto the pavement before ever I calls the Law to say he's
deid. He was seventy-four."

But she was looking more serious now. She didn't really
like Jack, but that didn't stop her asking his advice. She
was always friendly to people who might turn out to be
useful. A divorced mother had taught her that, by example.

When she thought, she put on a thinking face. She said
"Do I say 'yes' or 'no'?"

"He's okay. He's—how old are you?"

"Seventeen."

"Been out?"

"Yes."

"Well, then?"

She looked at the piece of paper again. After a long
while she said "I wish I could read his writing."

"He's asking you to supper."

"Tonight? I'm swimming."

"He means eleven o'clock."

"But everything's shut, eleven, isn't it?"

"In his chambers. That's like his flat. Official chambers."

"Oh?"

"Oh."

"Will you be there?" Sally asked.

"No."

"Will you be outside?"

"No."

"Will anybody else be there?"

"No."

"Will anybody else be outside?"

"No."

Sally Cohen smiled. Her cheek bones were high: a smooth, sweet, tough face. There was a suggestion of a dimple on the right side. "So tell him I'm coming," she said. Jack seemed pleased by her decision. He tipped back the brim of his cap, for a moment. He said of Julian, "He's got a sharp eye, I'll give him that."

"But tell him I'm swimming tomorrow and Saturday so I'm not staying late."

"I'll tell him." Then he stretched out his hand. "Now if I can have the letter?"

"What?" But she knew what he had asked. The red was already spreading up her brown cheeks.

"I said, if I can have the letter?"

"You cannot."

"Missie."

"This letter is addressed to me."

"If I can have it back, Miss. I'm serious."

He kept his hand outstretched and put on that expression with which men of no authority try to frighten other people. She made a little sick noise—an "ugh"—to indicate her disgust. She threw the letter back at him, turned and ran down the steps into the courtyard. She dropped her towel and costume, picked them up again, then walked off, self-consciously.

There aren't too many shops on Half Moon Lane, not the station end. Sally and all the Sallies walk up to Herne Hill, buy their milk, bread, coke, chips and chops there. Once, after an unnecessary row, Julian had sat in his un-likely expensive fast motor car, the yellow Dino, and watched her run from shop to shop. Maybe then they were both pretending they'd reach the only earthly goal of love, which is to live together; just live two for one; only that. Until it blows.

Now, in the rain, he had to stop the cab by the pillar box in front of the dairy. The lights were lit in those shops which weren't already closed this Saturday night. The wide road was more or less deserted, but it was a bleak and open place on which to be sick. The cabbie wanted to get home. Foolishly, Julian paid him off. He still had a quarter of a mile to walk down to Half Moon Lane. The cabbie didn't have the right change. He gained another bob; drove off.

Julian rested his shoulder against the pillar box. He knew he couldn't be very sick. There was no substance left. But he began to cough and retch and when his shoul-ders and head fell forward he felt he would never straighten them again. There was no booze shop, but a licensed grocer next to the dairy was still open.

The pavement seemed a mile wide because the claws were in him low down again. He hated them more than ever before. While the claws gripped he couldn't go into

Sally's. That was part of the game: maybe the whole game.

In the shop he leaned his left hip hard against the counter, trying to get some relief, then feared he was going to collapse. There was a high wooden, cane-seated chair, and while someone else was being served he sat there and tried to keep his eyes open. The rain had soaked him again. It must have taken him five minutes from the cab to the shop. The raindrops fell down his face. He liked it when they touched his lips.

A woman with a cleft palate had to talk to him three times before he understood that she was the shop assistant. He ordered some lemons and half a bottle of vodka; any lemon, thank you; any vodka. His money had got wet, somehow. He thought he'd lost it all, at first, but found it in the inside pocket of his overcoat.

He wanted to ring for another cab to take him down the road, but that was somehow impossible. It was less than a quarter of a mile. It was downhill all the way.

"You're all right, sir?"

In South London there must be nothing wrong with him, nothing ever, nothing at all, no pain. That was the first rule of the game.

"Sure?" some kind chap asked, again. Many men and women seemed to recognize and react kindly to his pain. They usually had some story to tell.

"All right?"

"Absolutely," Julian said. "Just a little drunk."

The hissing whisper in which he answered shocked no one. Nor did it convince them. Perhaps they thought "crime" or "spy" or more closely, "drugs". But most of them recognized death. They only pretended to believe him.

Outside, the pain grew worse. He reached the end of the row of shops, only about fifty yards, before he had to rest again. He was about to fall on his knees when he saw the low brick wall of the first house in the terrace that ran down to Half Moon Lane.

He didn't drink the vodka. He took a swig from the bottle with the green opaque liquid inside. Just a touch of the old jungle-juice, what could be nicer than that.

Then he bit into a lemon. He ravaged it, tore it about as if he intended to hurt it, to extract its guts. It dropped on the pavement and rolled down into the gutter; became, at once, black.

The street lights were switched on at that second. Very carefully he replaced the stopper in the jungle-juice and shoved it back in his coat pocket. It was a splendid coat. A very thick, grey coat that was shiny; a little shiny and not so dark when it wasn't like this, soaking wet.

It was too wet to light a cigar. But he tried. And tried. Again tried, muttering "Let go your claw, crab."

A hundred years ago, or was it only fifteen months, she, Sally as she then was, friend to the Duke and enemy of the Monarch—she swam at Holborn and again at Croydon. She was picked to compete at Hampstead after all. She told everyone at lunchtime in the sunny, dirty court-yard outside the office; "If only I could stop biting my nails."

And after the match she emerged from the girls' changing room, into the corridor, downstairs. The place was rather dark and voices echoed down it from the small pool. She took a moment to grow accustomed to the dim light.

"Hello. Oh it's you. I didn't recognize you in this light." There was no furniture. The floor was the same as the walls. It was a meeting in concrete, and Julian, for a moment, seemed at a loss for words.

"I saw you swim," he managed, at last.

"Did you. I bet you never thought I'd win."

She'd wrapped a towel round her; a yellow towel that made her skin look brown. It wasn't a very big towel.

She said "I was four seconds behind Judy until the last turn. I didn't think I'd do it myself."

He hadn't envisaged meeting her here in an open concrete place with noises from the children in the second pool.

"Then I did win," she said.

"I saw."

"You know this makes me almost a certain chance to try for the National in Brum? I shall be famous, don't you see? 'There goes Sally Cohen, the comet from 'Alf Moon Lane'...H—alf...I'm not sure you're really allowed round the back here. Anyway I'm not sure I want to speak to you."

Never, Julian was thinking, never in my whole life have I wanted, in the sense of physically desired, any person or thing as much as ...

And "It's your being in clothes," she said as he took her open mouth. It tasted still of chlorine.

"Not here, not here." Not here, in this open echo chamber. She was staring at him, then, asking "Why did you ask for your letter back?"

He wondered if it were her reaction to Jack-the-care-

taker that had hooked him. He asked, still staring at her
shoulders, neck, mouth, at the first curve of breasts that
needed no support, "Which letter?"

"You know which."

The towel hardly covered her decently. Not here.
"Not here, much as I like it, please, and I do, I don't like
young men. They don't know what to do, not really. But
I'm not going to." She twisted away. Her legs were brown
and smooth the whole way up, absolutely smooth until
suddenly . . .

"Not here or any place unless you explain that, about
the letter. Why didn't you trust me?"

Her eyes were in shadow. Her brow looked broad and
by her jet black eyebrows, almost swollen or bruised.
"Never," Julian was still thinking; "never anyone as
much as this. And six months ago, I took myself for dead.
How we are blessed."

She was asking "What kind of girl would I be to show
anyone else a letter like that?"

"I didn't tell the man to ask for the letter back."

The point seemed to be very important to her. She put
her arms round his neck. She stood on tiptoe to do so.
Very urgently, she asked "Promise?"

"Yes."

She stared into his face. "I don't believe you."

He said "Of course I didn't. He just thought it
might be wise to protect an idiot like me in his obsession."

"Obsession for what?" She smiled slowly. So did he.
Then very swiftly, before he could demonstrate in particular the area of his obsession, she dodged away. She was
very quick in her physical reactions, as if she'd been

ducking schoolmasters' blows all her days. Her laughter ran down the tunnel to the pool.

Oh crab, release your claw. Crab, I am defeating you, this once. I am where you said I would never be. I am at the corner of Half Moon Lane, and your hold is slackening. I can move. I shall reach her door. Crab, you are immersed in jungle-juice. Lie low.

In those early days, she didn't have the digs in Half Moon Lane. She lived with her mother and kid sister and stepfather, Den. He was a good man, younger than her mother.

She liked him. Den was a chemist, trained, she said. He worked in Bell and Croyden, assistant in the dispensary there. He was ever so anxious, thin on top, kind eyes and no spare flesh on him at all. It was awful, sometimes, how her mother bullied Den. Week-ends, he had to do everything for Julia, the five-year-old. They lived in a flat, in one of those new blocks that sweat inside, and not unlike the one that fell down in a heap, the other day. But Den was nice.

"Den?"

"Hello." It was a Croydon number. And she was phoning from Hampstead.

"It's me, Sally, I'm in a box." She could hear Julia behind him, kicking up a row. "What's the matter with her?"

"She won't eat her tea," Den said.

"Well, forget it. Bung it back in the fridge. She'll get hungry."

"I think something may have upset her . . ."

"Oh Den, really," Sally said. "She's perfectly all right. She's just a monkey, why can't you see that? Where's Mum?"

"She's not home yet."

Funny.

"Den, I've got a favour to ask."

"Oh yes?"

"Guess what. Clever me."

"You won the swimming?"

"Yes."

"The individual?"

"Yes."

"Oh, good on you, Sally, I am glad. I do congratulate you. Pam'll be ever so pleased about that. I'll tell her soon as she's in, we'll have a celebration. What d'you want to eat, then?"

"Den, that's it. I want to go have supper with Judy."

"With who?"

"My team-mate. Judy. You know." She lied in detail, always. "Her brother's home from the Marines but her parents are there too. It's all right."

"You better ring back about that, Sal."

"Tut."

"Sal, you know what she's like when—"

"I want to go right away. I won't be late. I got my key. You tell her."

"I don't like to."

"Oh, Den."

"What'll I say?"

"Just say how I'm the big champion at Hampstead, maybe get my face in the papers and I'm ever so happy and invited out to supper, isn't she proud?"

"Well."

"Go on."

"All right, Sal. Be good."

"Thanks, Den."

She paid no attention to the woman outside the box: she was old. She dialled again, the number Julian had given her, not the number of his digs or chambers or whatever but the number of a hotel, quite a swish hotel, as a matter of fact. She asked for the room.

"It's me," she said.

She said "I've made up my mind."

She said "No. You come down to the bar."

She said "Of course. I'm dying to."

When she put down the receiver she stood for a second biting the knuckle of her thumb. She wasn't thinking about her mother, or Den. There was another little fire at the back of her eyes. She was thinking of Cyn-thea Bell in Central Filing, the department's graad-you-ate. She was thinking, what if Cynthia knew. That made her smile.

And Julian's wife Christabel should have seen that dark, hard, competitive look. Sally never swam to lose.

Early in May is no time to die, not even in Half Moon Lane. He rang the door bell for the third time. The milk had all been taken in but there was no light from the front parlour, where the girls kept the TV and the discs and all their strange souvenirs: teddy bears, swimming cups and coronation mugs.

Sid answered at last. He didn't seem too surprised. Didn't see the pain in the eyes.

"Don't think she's in. You can try," he said, and bounded back upstairs, two at a time. Sid was studying to be a chartered accountant, but his next-door neighbour on the second floor was a bus conductor and happy at that.

Julian looked in the parlour. He switched on the ghastly overhead light and saw the chaos. The cushions off the modern settee were on the floor by the electric fire which was a sign that someone had been making love. Maybe Jacky. Maybe not Jacky; and there were only the two girls.

Oh, the games. Nobody could have guessed what drove the economist to Half Moon Lane that wet Saturday night.

He wandered into the cold room, where all the tin lids were filled with cigarette butts. He sat on an upright chair by the table which was never used because the kitchen led off the girls' bedroom at the back of the house. There was a rubber-plant in a pot but it was dead, or nearly dead.

There was a cutting from a French newspaper with a photograph of a blond Californian boy. He was wearing a parachute harness and an oxygen cylinder. He was a pioneer of the new sport, a sky diver, or space walker. He was called Josh Reynolds and he and his friends would fall seven or eight thousand feet before pulling the rip-cord. The oxygen jet allowed them to manoeuvre in the air. The French journalists had gone to town in the way only French journalists do: they could bring philosophy into pig farming. They said that Mr Reynolds's compulsion to fly without wings was yet another hidden protest against present conditions, an extreme blow connected to prevalent urbanization; said that space was his reality: the big trip. He looked brown and handsome, Sally's beau.

Brown and handsome and courageous and confident and Californian and shallow and absolutely right for Sally. Maybe he was in the back room. Maybe Jacky had moved upstairs to sleep with one of the boys or maybe she was there too, either alone or with another space walker. You know what divers are.

With a flash, a beautiful flash of living heartfelt pain, Julian pictured Sally naked, here at some orgy, or on a "trip", whatever it was called. But it is extraordinary how wildly inaccurate we are, in jealousy. We cannot see the loved one and her lover as the people that they are. We have not the stability or courage to build the scenes up logically. Instead we imagine exactly the same love scenes which we ourselves remember so well and simply superimpose the new character in our place. The imposition is ridiculous. The new character in no way resembles ourselves, therefore the scenes could never happen that way. Or, alternatively, we see the loved one behaving in some completely novel, brazen manner. She is doing things with him that she never would have done before. She has become more demonstrative, hungrier for passion; and lies panting, each time, more fully satisfied. It escapes us that she is still the same girl. That she doesn't change overnight; she can't.

Jealousy is wild and filthy, we know; is demanding, obsessive, leading always to thoughts of violence; but Lord, it is a living emotion. We are never more totally alive than when the loved one is lying in someone else's arms.

Julian had to sit down again. He did not tear up the cutting. He put it in his pocket. He would tell her he had torn it up. She would pretend not to care, say, sour grapes, that it wasn't a very good photo anyway. He would show her that he still had it, tease her with it, make a whole scene and prolong it until it ended in her tears. The loser has to make the scenes, has to raise the temperature to screaming pitch, because that is the only way he can penetrate and exhaust. The loser starts the rows and then holds on to them, going over the ground again and again. That's all that is left to him. Some husbands do it for years. There is no cure. They are only crying for the past. Maybe crying for something even more impossible: for a return to a passionate love of a pitch which never truly existed, but has been built up in their minds.

The past: the swish hotel that wasn't very swish ... By eleven o'clock, that very first time, she fell asleep. She snored which should have been an unendearing thing. But she snored like a child, not a drunk. The younger the girl, the simpler the underwear. Bra and pants, not even matching, lay on the floor. Julian picked them up as he wandered into the bathroom and ran the shower.

She woke suddenly, in confusion, screaming, just before he stepped under the shower. He dashed back to her bedside. She was very hot. He brushed her hair from her wet brow and gently kissed the moisture from her lips, her jaw, her neck. Even in those days he knew about semi-waking in panic, from poisoned dreams. He'd walked farther than most men through those woods.

"I didn't know where I was," she said, looking round the room at anonymous furniture.

He just held her together, by the shoulders. She looked at him as if he'd been with her all her life. The mascara was smudged on her eyes. At last she said "I feel stiff. Ouch."

"From the swimming."

She was already recovering herself. "My eye ... What's the time?"

"Eleven."

"Doom," she said. "Poor old Den. He'll be getting it from Mum. I had a horrid dream. That's not fair, is it?"

He noticed "You have had an operation. An appendix," and she grunted and pulled the sheet back over her. She turned her face away and lay still on the pillow. She was shy. She blushed. She smiled. She hung onto the sheet, gripping it very tightly, saying "No" when he tried to pull it away. She wrapped it round her as she rolled back to ask "Did I say something in my sleep?"

"As you were waking."

"What?"

He didn't reply directly. Instead, he asked "Have you done this before? Answer, Yes."

"What ever did I say?" She sat up. "No, tell me."

She'd called out some name as she awoke. She'd closed her chunky little fist and banged the empty place beside her on the bed. She'd cried out the name, with her eyes wide open, several times.

He said "It sounded like George."

"I don't know any Georges."

"Then let's say it was Julian."

"Oh? Not Julian," she said. "Julia. I don't think of you as Julian. I might have said Julia. She's my sister. The little one who lives at home. She's sweet, but they spoil her. Den worships her. I'm the only one that tells her off. And yet I think she respects me for it. I don't know what they'll do when I leave. I'm the only one can shut her up."

She talked as if she were connected to him for life. She talked as if they had arrived and that was that. Inconsistently, then, she no longer objected to him loosening the sheet round her as she protested, "I promise, Julia always gets into my bed. Don't you believe me? Specially Sunday morning. And if she wakes in the night. She sleeps in the same room. Don't you believe me, then?"

He said he did, why shouldn't he?

She fell sideways on the bed, and moaned, saying again how tired she was. She started slowly to bring one arm over, then the next, turning her wrist inward in a lazy, classy, slow-motion crawl. Laughing and groaning.

Then she let her head drop. She said "Yes, I've done it before. But I've never come through." Such a little hook.

"You mean, not until tonight?"

"I didn't tonight."

"But, my darling—"

"I know I was biting, scratching. Maybe that's why."

She lay quite still until he kissed the nape of her neck, by way of a promise. He hadn't intended to do more. But she turned, uncovered by the sheet; naked; turned right over, not shy at all, any more, one leg flat on the bed, the other bent at the knee, rocking to and fro. She had a strong, new smell which Julian could only then describe to himself as young and also un-Christabel. She wasn't a big girl but she was very strong and firm. She cupped a hand round his chin suddenly and turned his face to one side. That was no child's gesture. Buried in the child, so to speak, was a woman, a European woman.

She said "I'm an aristocrat really. Look at my second toe."

She said "I may look Spanish, but I asked Mum and she said we're Russian really, somewhere or was."

She said "You've got a super, super face. How d'you get those rings round your eyes? Inside, I mean? They're a sign of temper, meant to be."

"They are."

"Will you beat me up?"

"Yes."

"Do you promise?"

Their smiles faded away. She looked at him so hard and searchingly that she almost squinted. Yet she seemed to seek no answer. She stretched up her arms and put them round his neck. She'd found an appetite that fed upon itself. And at the same time she said kindly "Don't worry, old man, I don't trust you an inch."

Recovering, around midnight she traced the scar round his chest very gently with her finger. "They didn't half carve you up" was all she said. It was the only time she ever referred to his illness.

And it was several months later when she first asked about his wife.

"What's she called?"

She asked that in Brighton, one sunny morning. She didn't tell him, but she'd come through, and she was happy about that.

"Who?"

"You know who."

"Christabel."

"Thats' nice. Has she been faithful to you?"

"Not absolutely."

She didn't like him when he was Oxford like that.

"What's 'not absolutely'?"

"Not absolutely," very coldly.

"Okay," she said softly, then yelled, as he was about to respond: "OKAY!"

She was working at some holiday camp, at that time, teaching kids how not to drown. She wore a blazer with

brass buttons and she was supposed to put on a red cap.
She looked very pretty in it, to everybody else, but for
some reason it made her feel a fool.

But she was wearing it as she ran all the way to the
station, to surprise him, the day he had to go. At the time,
he found her almost embarrassing. She didn't cry. She
never did. But she hung on to his wrist. She picked at
his watch. She flung her arms round his neck and stood
on tiptoe. She laughed because his hair was beginning to
go grey; it glinted in the sun. She tried to explain about
some pompous swimming instructor who had corrected
her, that morning. She showed him a paragraph she had
found about the Cabinet Office. His name wasn't even
mentioned in it. She said "Nobody would guess there's
ordinary people in it, I mean someone like you." She was
proud of the fact that he was important, was *someone*, but
at the same time more proud that he wasn't stuck-up. She
loved him for not being extraordinary—or ordinary except
for the fact that he'd rings round the pupils of his eyes.
She folded the cutting in her fist. She said "When I'd
nothing to do after this instructor bawled me out I went
in the office and sulked and cut off some hair."

"Where?" he asked.

She understood the innuendo, and instinctively ignored
it. She seemed to be born with an inner knowledge of all
men's games. She just pointed to a patch behind her ear.

He forgot to ask for the lock of hair. Lord, what arro-
gance.

She was devastated. "Oh hell."

"Darling, of course I'd love to have it."

"No you wouldn't."

"Please."

She gave it to him, reluctantly, sulkily. When he took it she shouted angrily in his face "Don't you bloody well laugh."

"I'm not laughing."

She said, like a gypsy, "If you throw it away I wish you bad luck for the rest of your life."

She didn't say she loved him because in the books—or maybe it was her sister Shelley who told her—they advise against saying it outright, first, if you're the girl. He didn't say he loved her. He didn't know if he did.

When at last the train left she ran out to the car park and sat on the wall in the sun, pretending that the glare hurt her eyes. She didn't own dark glasses, in those days.

A big American boy who was carrying a kit bag and an oxygen cylinder approached her. He was tall, nervous, restive and pushy, and she wasn't friendly, at first.

But he was also cheerful.

He said "Oh, come on, Clementine, big brother's not going to eat you. I seen you saying good-bye to Dad."

"He's not Dad."

"I know he's not Dad. So I give you a drink."

"I don't drink."

"But you've never had a Bloody Mary . . . with lemon, celery salt."

"All right."

For some reason she showed the young man the crumpled cutting about the Cabinet Office. He was nice about that.

"He must be high on I.Q."

She didn't really understand that. In fact she didn't properly understand most of the things he said. He talked in a hippy kind of code, or in abstract phrases which were

above her head, most of the time. She talked of Julian.
Said she was sorry, then talked of him again.

"That is some hang-up," Josh Reynolds said.

When Julian awoke again, it took him a moment to get
his bearings. He never knew whether it was the drug or
the illness itself which made such a nonsense of time and
waking and sleeping. Dreams and memories encroached
upon each other and together invaded reality: there was
never any rest.

He still had the cutting about Josh Reynolds in his
hand. The light was glaring, overhead, but the house was
silent. It seemed like the middle of the night.

Pain had been worse, much worse than this. He decided
to go through to the bedroom and wake up Sally's friend
Jacky, but there's a hopeless lag between decision and
action, at this late stage.

He sat still, trying not to become confused, but to remember clearly the good times.

Months before, in the heart of the good times, a week
or two after Sally came back from Brighton, he had
woken Jacky up . . . No. He was wearing a coat then, too,
so it must have been later in the year, maybe closer to
Christmas when all mistresses retire to their families and
see themselves as children see them: painted aunts upon a
painted shelf. At which point Josh Reynolds had arrived
by oxygen-driven reindeer through the sky.

But the first talk with Jacky was before Reynolds had
become any sort of reality. And it was a good talk, because
Julian knew almost as much about Jacky as he did about
baby sister Julia. After love, it was Sally's habit to discuss

Jacky's teeth, or her boy friends, the current fiancé (an altogether different matter), her father, who was a comedian, her untidiness, her job as sole secretary to an Import-Export Arab, her gynaecological difficulties, her hatred of the smell of fish, her ability to wake up in the morning or her chronic failure to reach an orgasm with everyone except a brewer's drayman who had once met her in a roadside café near East Grinstead and invited her simply: "All right then Shorty, round the back."

On this Christmas occasion, Julian remembered, Jacky's bedroom door was unlocked. He sat on her bed.

"It's me. Julian. Sally's Julian."

"Oh?" Jacky was hardly awake.

"Where is she?"

"She will be disappointed. She's out."

"When will she be back?"

Jacky woke up, a bit more. She asked "Are you drunk, then?"

"No."

"She says you drink ever so much."

"She says you fuck ever so much."

"Does she?" Jacky asked, then added "It's that nice Oxford way you say it makes it sound worse. She says your language surprises."

"Why are you in bed?"

"Because I sleep in bed."

"Alone?"

"Because I have been removing hair almost painlessly. Sal bought it, like hot wax. Funny how she don't have any hair on her thighs isn't it?"

"She has on her wrists."

"Yes she has lots, and a bit on her tummy."

"Very little. Very downy. It's nice."

"Is it?"

He asked "Did she tell you that I had hair on my chest?"

"Yes," she answered, "as a matter of fact she did, amongst other details that could hang the whole of Downing Street, I'd think. Do you want some coffee?"

"Yes."

She used to wear all Sally's clothes and stretch them. That went for nighties too.

As she stepped out of the bed she revealed thighs pink from the pain of the wax.

"Oh dear," she said, "it's all that meat."

She treated Julian as if he had slept in the same room all his life. She was completely unshy and unworried by his presence. He lay back on Sally's bed which was only two and a half feet wide. It squeaked. In that dingy, cleaned once a fortnight, chaotic, next-to-the-kitchen, room.

Jacky said "She'll be savage, missing you like this."

"I can wait."

"What about Christabel? Is she in the country?"

"Yes."

"I thought you had an important dinner, tonight, in the corridors of power."

"I walked out."

"Fancy."

"How's Ron?"

"Who's Ron?"

"Your fiancé."

"Oh, him. He's all right, I expect."

"And what about Sid?"

"I've gone off Sid. You take sugar?"

"No."

"You'll have to do with dried milk. It was my turn to go to the dairy."

"How's export-import?"

"It's all right. I wish you could do without C forms and all those bills of lading stuff. Go tell Harold that, would you, on Jacqueline's behalf."

"Jacky, this can't go on. It was one thing for a month or two. But I'm in danger of getting badly hooked."

"How condescending can you get."

"It's getting out of control."

"All right then. Break her heart. You will, if you walk out. You don't know what you are in Sal's life."

She gave him his coffee.

He said "It's better now, before Christmas."

She interrupted. "I told you. Break her heart . . . Here she is, now."

The front door slammed. Her footsteps. She had been across at her mother's putting Julia to bed. She wasn't at her best. She was just a girl in Half Moon Lane.

"Oh darling—" her whole face lit up when she saw him. She flung her coat away and dived onto the bed.

"Jacky, don't go. Where'll you go?"

"Sid, I expect."

The memory of Sally's smile reassured Julian for a moment, and he managed to tuck the Josh Reynolds cutting away. He got to his feet and stretched his back and felt a little stronger: strong enough to go and invade the back bedroom. But Jacky wasn't so forthcoming, now. Had she known the agony that he had surmounted to reach the room, in the first place, she might have behaved differently. In fact, she treated him much as she might have had he been an official of the Gestapo known for his moderation.

She was polite enough. "Sorry, I didn't hear you knock."

He had sat down on Sally's bed: on the dirty red counterpane.

He said "It's coffee time again."

"You must think I spend my whole time in bed."

"Just a large part of it."

But she too had changed. "That's all over," she said, "I'm engaged."

"So you were before."

"Officially engaged."

"To Ron."

"Ron? No, no. To Bill."

He asked "Is Sally engaged?" He knew the answer was "yes".

"She's back from France. She's been to France with him, did you know?" He hadn't known. Jacky was quick to see it. She changed the subject rapidly: "You're soaked, aren't you? That's why you're shivering."

"Did she have a good time in France?"

"She's quite brown. The weather was nice, she says. I don't like the French, do you?"

"What about the Americans?"

She had climbed out of bed. She looked at him quite hard. She said "I'm not playing any of your games. No doubt you're cleverer 'an I am, Julian, so I'm not playing word games because I don't want to be catched out. All right?"

Julian nodded. He put his elbow on his knee and rested his brow in his hand. He put the cigar down in an ashtray on Sally's bedside table, on which rested her clock, some awful novel which he had not given her, two dirty cups, a second ashtray bought in Brighton, a hairbrush and comb, and a signed coloured photograph of Mr J. Reynolds 10,000 feet off the ground, with the parachute still in the pack. That picture had been on the cover of an international magazine. And it hurt.

Julian looked at it very carefully and thought "Yes, crab, it hurts. All is well. It still hurts. And the thought of her French idyll, that also hurts. Not very much, not enough to quiet your raking claw, but I do feel it hurt."

Jacky said "I'll put a spot of whisky in your coffee. We got some Old Grandad."

After a pause he answered ironically "American whisky? Now that would be nice."

"I didn't mean it that way. Honest. It's just—"

"I've never met Mr Reynolds. What's he like?"

"Oh. Josh? Well. He's not married. You must see that."

"Do you like him?"

"We've never fancied the same man, Sal and I."

"Is she with him tonight?"

Jacky buttoned up: "You'll have to ask her that."

"If he left her, would it break her heart?"

"Did you want this whisky, then?"

"Yes, please."

After a while Jacky said "I'm leaving next week. I'm off. She's going to be my bridesmaid come September. I'm living at home again until then. I have to save up."

Julian said "You don't really like him, do you?"

"I didn't say that."

And to Sally, when at last she came home, he said "The last time you came in here you dived on the bed."

This time she did not smile.

"I'm soaked through, give me a chance. And you've no right coming here without ringing, I told you that. Where on earth have you been?"

"I've been at the hotel. I had a Cutty Sark. The barman sends his love."

"That's nice. But you can't stay. I've got to go to Glasgow tomorrow. I'm swimming in the Jansen Cup. I'm not having any dramatics, Julian. I don't want a late night. I've got to go first thing, tomorrow, really I should be there tonight."

He thought, if she uses that same cool voice once again, I'll finish it there. I'll walk into the kitchen, I can manage to walk into the kitchen, and I shall take the carving knife.

She said "You go back to bed, Jacky, catching your death. She's had flu. Trust her to get something the moment I walk out for my French holiday." She smiled—about the only time she smiled—then added "If that's not a dirty word."

Jacky said she'd try and get a bed upstairs.

"No," Sally replied.

"Well, I'll watch telly through in the front."

"No you will not. We'll go through there. Come on, Julian. Oh God. Look at the mess you've made. Look, the bed's all wet. It's off your coat. Come on."

She pulled him by the hand, not as if she wanted to

touch his hand. He said "I was admiring your bedside photograph."

"Yes. In'it something? Everyone thinks it must be taken by another diver but actually it's over Phoenix and it was taken with a telescopic lens from a B.57."

"Oh, shit," Julian said.

"Language. And close that door."

In the parlour the old pain returned. A boy came downstairs who was neither Sid nor Simon. He wanted to watch some late-night sports report, to see some European Cup football match. It seemed to Julian that Sally had reverted to behaviour like her mother's, not that he had met her mother. She kept doing the right thing. She corrected Julian for swearing; she introduced him, in full, to this boy from upstairs. She explained who the boy was, and what he was doing: some kind of electrical engineering apprenticeship.

She tidied up the room, and seemed angry that Jacky and Bill had left the cushions on the floor.

He said "I thought you'd left them there. You and your American friend."

She behaved as if she had never lain on that floor stripped from the waist down saying "Christ, I like it on the floor." She pretended she hadn't heard him.

He persisted "Wasn't it you?" and she turned and glowered at him; glowered in exactly the same manner that an adolescent sister glowers at her younger brother when he reveals some intimate truth... "I'm warning you—" said her lowered brow.

The boy couldn't have been less interested in their conversation, nor did the sight of Sally's legs seem to impress him. She looked horribly affected as she picked up the cushions and put them back in place. She hummed as she stacked all the long-playing records together. She complained about Jacky again. She emptied ashtrays. She readjusted her hair and said "It's longer, do you like it?" But, in truth, with every movement and intonation she said one thing, only one thing: "You are not my keeper now. I can ignore your likes and dislikes, I can behave absolutely as I please. I can forget all you taught me as I want to forget, WANT to forget the pleasure and passion that we had."

Then she sat down beside him, clasped his hand firmly and said "My poor darling, you're trembling. You probably caught Jacky's flu. Did you make a pass at her, in there?"

He thought "I'll kill her, why not?"

Meantime, the Cup game grew more exciting. There was to be extra time. The boy lost his electrical engineering cool for a moment and said "Knock-out". He lit up a pipe.

"I love the smell of pipes," Sally said, patly. Slowly, Julian began to giggle and nearly to cry. He reached in his pocket for the vodka and thought of his wife, his excellent wife. He thought "Oh Christabel, were you to know the extent of your victory, were you to see my stupidity and humiliation." And the crab squeezed a long, low, low squeeze. He thought, Lord, I mustn't die here, watching the telly from the three-piece, not with this kind of prissy companion.

Sally said "Hey, what about me?" and took the vodka flask. "D'you mind if I pour some in a glass?"

"Go on talking," Julian prayed, "go on being awful

and false and common and I will get out of here, get home and die, if I must, in peace."

But it wasn't to be that way. Only twelve hours later they were to be found in Glasgow: he, Sally and Christabel. All three. All hell let loose.

Chapter Two

CHRISTABEL was a very pretty girl with thick blond hair which fell over her face. In public she ate nuts and drank champagne. Lord knows what she ate in private, because she wasn't thin. She was extremely nervous and moved very rapidly. She laughed a great deal in company, maybe because she was so shy.

If you watch the sea on a cloudy day, you may become awed by its infinite invention. Not only does its colour constantly change within the range of blue, grey and green but waves form and break without the pattern ever being repeated. Nervous children, it is said, can be re-orientated by a few days on a beach. The sea both fascinates and reassures them. We are talking of Christabel's eyes.

She had a past. She was married to an absurd motor-racing lord until she fell in love with Julian. Before that, in a kind of social agitation, she slept with several under-graduates and an old don who said of her, when she was still sixteen, that in bed she was a merry old soul. She was badly educated; she was a champion skier; she gobbled up book after book; she was almost pathologically extravagant; she burnt the candle at both ends; she ran until she dropped. She was highly intelligent.

Thirty-six hours after Julian's extraordinary last pil-grimage to Half Moon Lane, she was to be found, of all places, in a cafeteria in Nile Street, Glasgow, at 8.0 a.m. About twenty hours had passed since the worst series of scenes in her life, one in London, one on an Anglo-Scottish flight to Glasgow, one at a swimming-pool in Glasgow. She still felt washed out; stunned. She had to wait until the water boiled before she was served with a cup of instant coffee. She bought a ham roll and only ate a bite of it. She sat in the corner of this big, low basement room of peculiarly Scottish texture: formica, tartan, linoleum and carbohydrate.

Other morning Glasgow people with doughy com-plexions and coaly shadows under their eyes sat down on the awkward little benches and seats, all round her. They took starch to sustain them on their way to work and most noticeably, incessantly, they talked to each other. Vaguely, because she was in a state of almost complete disjunction, it occurred to Christabel that these lonely people must all have been acquainted with each other. But listening care-fully she discovered that this was not so. They merely addressed each other as acquaintances in the way extras used to do in Ealing films about the war. They were bound together in a common tragedy: they lived and worked in this black city.

"Hello, there, and how's Glasgow treating you?"

To the best of her knowledge and belief, Christabel had never seen the young man before.

"Can I sit down beside you, said the spider to the fly?"

"Please," Christabel said nervously. He was a most peculiar looking man. He was over six foot tall, skinny and bespectacled. He had crinkles in his hair that spread all over his face. He looked not unlike a character in a comic cartoon who is the victim of a high voltage electric shock. The writing in the balloon above his head would have read "zzzzzzz-eee-ouch!"

He sat down and said "Come on now, dear, it can't be as bad as that."

Giggling, Christabel said "It is." Then she smoked some more, and for a second was serious. She said "You don't know", and poured some of the coffee in her saucer back into the plastic cup. Her hair had fallen forward as soon as the young man sat down. She used it as a screen.

"D'you not want that bap?" he asked.

"Bap?"

"Ham roll."

"Oh. Oh no."

He said "Thanks, dear," and Christabel thought "Ah, a Scotchman with an elementary motive."

As he said "Thanks" he held out his hand, not palm upwards as she might have expected, but sideways. She immediately placed the bitten bap in it. He completely dissolved in hysterical laughter, hissing some word that sounded like "Cheese". It took him half a minute to get it across to her that he had intended to shake hands.

Christabel pushed her hair aside and slowly smiled. She decided that he was a nice kind of Scotchman. She was feeling so weak after the most horrifying twenty-four hours of her life that she became infected with his laughter. Only a moment later, when the confusion had subsided did they manage to exchange names.

"Mozart Anderson," the Scotchman said. "Now shake a paw." He had taken off his glasses. Tears of laughter had misted them over.

He asked "Have you been in Glasgow before?"

"Never," she said, implying "and never again."

"Now don't be like that. It's a great place when you get to know it."

"I don't think I will."

"Are you going south today?"

"I don't know."

"By plane?"

"I don't know."

"D'you want some more coffee?"

"No."

"Yes," he said.

"All right, yes."

She lit another cigarette as he went back to the counter with her cup.

When he returned he said "I'm going to tell you about a public disgrace."

Christabel said "Oh yes?"

"A bloody downright injustice."

She withdrew the cup from her lip.

He asked "Too hot?"

She shook her head.

"I know," he said, condemning himself. "You don't take sugar?"

"It doesn't matter."

"I put an extra spoonful in. I thought you looked as though you needed glucose. Do you never take sugar?"

"It doesn't matter."

He seemed unhappy about it. But he returned to the first subject.

He said "How long do you think you have to be a referee for, before you take a first-class game?"

"I've really never put my mind to that subject," she replied. Candidly, she felt a little alarmed by Mr Anderson. And did Glasgow mothers really christen baby boys "Mozart" or "Beethoven"?

"Seven years," he said. "Seven long years."

"Gosh, that does seem a long time."

"And do you know how much a referee gets when he reaches seventh grade?"

"I don't know how he gets paid, I'm afraid."

"By the match."

"Fifty pounds?" she suggested.

"Excellent," he said. "That's the figure that would be near fair. In fact he gets less than half of that. With twenty or thirty thousand people watching, can you imagine? Can you imagine the responsibility? Blowing the whistle. Sending players back to the dressing-room. And d'you know what he gets for a second division game?"

"Less."

"Ten pounds. Ten. After five or six years. Now if that isn't a screaming injustice, I ask you, what is?"

"It doesn't sound too fair," she said.

Suddenly he took her cup out of her hand. "For Christ's sake, dear, I can't stand this. I'll get you one without sugar."

"No, please. I was just holding it. I don't want any more. Honestly."

"You're looking sad again."

She tried to smile. But didn't make it this time. For a split second she was afraid that she was going to cry.

"Is there no sign of them?" Mozart asked.

"I beg your pardon?"

"I asked 'Is there no sign of them, this morning?'"

She was confused, wondering if he were embarking on some Scotch riddle.

"I don't understand."

He paused for a moment, then he said "Your husband and that wee bitch, wee Sally Cohen?"

"You know her?" She was astounded.

Mozart had stood up to go and fetch the coffee. He seemed to understand that she was going to break down before she recognized the symptoms herself.

He said "You're going to need another coffee. You didn't sleep at all last night, did you?"

"That's nothing new."

"No, I don't know Sally Cohen..." Then he stopped. Something seemed to dawn on him. He said "Christ. I get it now. You don't recognize me, do you?"

"I'm sorry?"

For a second he sounded deeply offended. She thought, wrongly, that he was joking.

He said "What kind of man do you think I am?"

She giggled nervously.

He said "No. Do you think I'd just approach a woman like that?... In a teashop? Just come up? Just come up like that? Arthur Gigolo?... I was at the pool yesterday, I'm one of the judges, in a track suit. I saw that whole horrible scene, you, your husband and her. Also out in the hall, you and Sally Cohen."

She was nodding. Just nodding and nodding.

He went to fetch the coffee without sugar. As the waitress handed it to him a woman came and tugged his elbow and pointed back at the corner table.

Christabel was weeping. She had buried her head in her arms and she was shaking, uncontrollably.

He was marvellous with her. He isolated them: ushered everyone else out of the way. He treated her firmly and clinically as for shock. "Just let it happen for a wee bit longer. Just let it happen. Then hold up your head, woman, and take a sip of this."

"You are a very nice Scotchman" was the first thing Christabel managed to say. So then he took her out and put her in his motor car which was a filthy rusty old Ford, and drove her away.

"I think it was because you called her a bitch," Christabel said. "Thank God somebody did that."

It was sunny and warm when they reached Furbank.

"And who plays at Furbank?"

She said "You must stop asking me that kind of question, because I don't follow football."

"Partick Thistle play at Furbank. And who plays at Ibrox?"

"I've heard of Ibrox."

"Rangers play at Ibrox. And Celtic play at Parkhead or Parkheid, depending on your command of the argot. I have just introduced you to a whole new wonderful world."

The groundsmen seemed to know him.

He didn't take her to the grandstand, but led her all the way round to the north side. He sat her on the steps there.

He laid down his mac for her to sit on. There were two groundsmen working on the pitch by the far goal. Otherwise the place was deserted; and sheltered.

She said "It is really quite warm."

"I'll be one hour with these creeps."

"Arguing about seventh grade fees?"

"Very good," he said.

"Won't anyone object to me sitting here?"

"Not if you say you're a chum of Mozart Anderson's."

As he was about to leave, when he was two steps below her, beside one of the concrete "leans", she asked "Why do they call you Mozart?"

"Because I'm an expert on the clarinet."

"Really?"

"The best."

And off he went.

When he came back, she said, with wonder, "I fell asleep."

"That was the idea."

"What have you got there?"

His blazer pockets were bulging. He had half a bottle of gin, four baby tonics, some sandwiches in cellophane packs and two apples.

"Not forgetting the opener," he said.

"Good Lord, it's twelve o'clock. I must have slept for more than two hours."

"You did."

He wore floppy suede shoes that made his feet look dusty and enormous. He said "I love gin. I just love it. Don't you?"

*

He said "My wife walked out on me."

Ah. A Scotchman with a complex motive.

"I'm telling you," he said. "Don't you care?"

"Yes, go on," she answered.

"You don't care a rap. Only Glasgow people care."

"No. Go on."

"D'you know why you don't care a rap?"

"Because I'm selfish."

"Because you haven't had enough gin. If you finish that one right away before you eat the sandwiches then you'll be very very sympathetic to my sad tale."

She obeyed.

"All right," she said. "Your old woman walked out on you."

"Exactly. Twice."

"Ah."

"It's the 'twice', isn't it? It's the twice that hooks you?"

"Yes it is," she said.

She said "I'm waiting."

"She was and is a very bright girl, my wife. She is and was a journalist, feminist, John Osbornist, nationalist, columnist. The 'isms' were all part of what she took to bed and even there she did not spare herself in the struggle. She looked like a very very pretty woman who had just been in a punch-up. She went to Madrid to report on a match there when Celtic were on top: to comment on the scene, not the football. At Madrid airport she met an American film star who was not Kirk Douglas and he said 'I'm going to Seville, honey, to shoot some scenes on location.' She went with him and some kind friend mentioned this unimportant fact to me, here, at home in

Glasgow, working at the pool weekdays and Johnny Fifth Grade on Saturday afternoons."

"I'm listening."

"A-huh. You should take more gin now because I am about to behave toward my wife in a traditional and disgusting Scottish manner."

"You hit her?"

"No. No. You don't know how nasty we really are. When she came back with two hundred duty free cigarettes and several sexual bruises I was charming to her and said 'Let's go to the pictures', and I took her to a film in which this same actor was performing. That night she said how she was tired, so I let her sleep. She smelt of sunburn oil. The following evening I said 'There's another film I'd like to see.' So okay, she comes along with me. And funny, it's the same star."

"Christ," Christabel said. "Poor girl."

"A-huh. Well, I went on doing it. We saw eight films, all with this same star and I never made any comment and she never made any comment, then one night I come home from the pool and she's packed up and walked out and I broke up the furniture."

"You haven't seen her since?"

"No."

"D'you know where she is?"

"She's in Manchester."

"How long ago did she leave?"

"Four years ago."

"Do you still love her?"

"No."

The end of the story seemed to be something of an anticlimax. Again Christabel laughed and said "*Well*."

"I just love gin. I like to try and taste it through the tonic, don't you?"

"Oh Mozart," she said delightedly, "you are quite a find."

Chapter Three

WAKING from an eternity, at just about that time, and in a private hotel, not sixty miles away, Julian thought, confusedly, there is vomit in my mouth; thought "The central problem underlying the recurring crisis of the pound is a social one not economic, discuss"; thought, the pain is higher, there is a certain numbness below, the great big crab is lying asleep amongst the seaweed of my bowels, I dare not move; thought, Anglo-Scottish First Class, I came on a trip on an aeroplane, a wedding party was involved; thought, there is no end to the weapons we use to involve others in our pain; thought, my sons are rather timid little boys, not much like Christabel—I took one to watch a train rush and bang through Didcot station and he trembled and shook but cried not to be taken away until another train went through.

He reached out for a bell above the bed, as if he were back in hospital and somebody said "Darling".

Julian thought, Not Christabel.

"Darling, darling."

Thought, there is no pain, it is all numb, I am dead. I am dead. I am going. They cannot hear me. Crab, bite! Give me pain rather than this, they are letting me drift.

56

Thought, it isn't a farce, so don't drop the bloody curtains, it isn't a farce at this age, it's a damned serious
business, tug Christabel, Chris—

"Darling, it's me. It's Sally. Sally."

Sight came back slowly. The room began to take shape.
A wood room. Panelled in maple or pine. A pioneer's kind
of room with windows by the floor and a roof sloped
down against the snows. Thought, God Almighty, where
are we now?

"It's me, Sally."

Both her hands were round his yellow hand. She had
no veins like his. She was leaning forward and the gold
confirmation cross that hung round her neck was dangling
over their clasped hands.

Her wrist was dark and downy. She was wearing a
corduroy overcoat, unbuttoned. He took it all in very
slowly. A red pullover, with a turtle neck. Her face was
that of a refugee who is not afraid. The face of a girl who
has crossed the Ukraine. He could hear something. There
was a thumping like distant guns, a persistent thumping
that vibrated through the room. She gave him no explanation of the sound. He stared at her again as if she were a
stranger. A broad little face and a mouth with no lip-
stick on it. A short nose. Thick black hair pulled back
from a low brow, not lying shiny and feathery and short
like Sally's usually did. How they change in their looks;
in their hearts too, he thought. But the eyes were Sally's,
Sally's ten years from now, worn down by the responsibility and pain and hopelessness of an invalid's passion, do
not call it love: of an invalid's hook, his gaff.

He therefore told her gently "Get out, my darling
while you can."

"I'm here. I'm not going. Ever. We decided that yesterday." She did not brush his hair back from his face;
she shoved it. He felt the heel of her hand as she pressed it
against his brow.

"Again."

She pushed it again and again as if she were bringing
warmth and blood back to some cramped animal and he
thought—Give me your heart and your blood, somehow
press your jugular into my teeth, woman it is your life that
I want, woman within Sally, whoever you are, woman of
total courage and unfailing strength, keep me on this
earth, for Christ's sake, never again let me drift... The
snow was numb and quiet.

He was trembling, shaking, shaking, muttering about
the trains at Didcot station, and then there was too much
smoke from some imagined volcano, too many bright
sulphuric fumes for him to separate himself from his sons.

"You've been asleep for nearly four hours."

Crab? Where's crab? No crab.

She said "Whee-ooo, talk about saying things in your
sleep."

He found the strength to raise her hand to his mouth.
He traced the line of the muscle and the waist of it by her
wrist. Then he lifted it to his teeth.

He wanted it there forever.

"Hey," she smiled and pulled it away.

A wood room. Panelled in plank strips, with not too
many knots in the wood. Varnished. An awful old bed
and an odour of lavender and moth balls somehow out of
keeping with this male place. Also a fluffy white rug on
the floor.

"Canada?" he asked.

"Mm?"

"Are we in Canada? Or Russia?"

"We could be," she answered. "And in May. I have to wear this coat in here. We're in Scotland, old man. In bonny Lochearnhead."

"What's all the thumping?"

"Dancing."

"Oh yes."

He didn't understand, at all.

She smiled.

Then, for the first time, he invited her to play the game that Christabel knew so well. It was a game that seemed to come out of his eyes; to emerge suddenly and dangerously like a Chinese dragon through the rings that circled his extraordinary pupils.

"Why are you here?" he asked quietly.

She looked quite mystified. "What d'you mean 'why'?"

"Why are you, a young girl, wasting your time with this cripple?"

Had Christabel been in Sally's shoes she would have at once been on her guard; would have answered with care "You're not a cripple." Would have continued, perhaps: "I decided. I left my Californian boy friend. You're sleepy, but you'll remember." Would have explained: "There were some scenes with your wife at Half Moon Lane, then all three of us came up to Scotland on an Anglo-Scottish champagne flight. We got involved with a wedding party. Then you came to the pool, don't you remember? There was a scene at the pool."

But not Sally. What she didn't understand, especially if it were said in a tone that sounded unloving, she instantly dismissed.

She said "Hey, I've been looking in my diary while you've been asleep."

He shook his head. He felt too weak to laugh at her irrelevance.

She said "D'you know you once made love with me in the middle of the night without my knowing it?"

"Then how do you know now?"

"Well, I've got it here in my diary."

"But how could you know to put it in your diary?"

"Because you told me, silly. On the night of October 21st. It was a Friday. It was often Fridays that patch." She smiled. "Nice."

Sally had never starved. None of the kids have starved. Her father was in the R.A.F. with all those proper allowances, and even before Den arrived on the scene, ends met. Yet there was something about her nature associated with poverty. The strange, slummy mixture of toughness and sugar separated her even from Jacky. It was as if she had inherited a knowledge of want. It haunted her at night, maybe leading to those extraordinary, violent noisy nightmares; it kept her asleep, soundly and determinedly asleep in the morning sun. Even in her sleep—why, especially in her sleep—she made the best of the warmth; she drank in the present when the present was good. Then there were sudden blank moments; sudden dark and inexplicable clouds such as we only see on the faces of very young children whose dumb sadness moves every one of us: we don't know what hurts them.

Paradoxically, she also treasured memories. She kept things: cuttings, tickets, champagne corks, letters, locks of hair, snapshots, badges. She always wrote up her diary and very often turned over the pages of the months gone by. Much of her conversation with Julian was devoted to remembrance of happy times they had experienced before.

During such recollections she was less honest than the rest of us. She never put bad things in her diary. It is the poor girl who looks back on the tiniest patch of sunlight, really no more than an hour's relief from the struggle and pain; she makes a summer of it.

To sentimentalize Sally in this way is to take away from Julian. He wasn't so silly as to make something out of her which she was not; to impose upon her the characteristics of some Liza of Lambeth. Her tendency to sentimentality was a real thing. It did not rule her life. On the contrary, she grabbed as fast as anyone. But she liked sentimental moments just as she liked rum and Coca Cola. They were her pleasure. She never looked back with sadness. It was always "That was a super day" or "I was in love with you by that time, yes, because I remember at the turnstile coming out of the pool I couldn't see you and I thought Oh Christ he's had to go back to Christabel."

She has nothing, Julian often told himself at times like this, nothing beyond her youth. The sorrow lies in her own awareness of that fact. She knew these to be her years; her short years; her life.

Maybe because he feared for her he said, rather cruelly, "You don't even listen to half the things I say. Half the things anybody says."

"Who's talking? You're always switching off. More than half an hour each side of the time you make love to me you're always switched off. For instance what's my sister's name?"

"Julia."

"And the other?"

"Shelley."

"And Julia's father?"

"Den."

"I don't know how you do it," she said. "We'd a girl like you at school. She used to sit at the back doodling and reading books and worse than that and everything the teacher said went right into her head. But she had acne."

"I haven't got acne."

"No, you haven't. You've got a lovely, super yellow face." She touched it and added, with brilliance, "as old as a Chinaman."

Chapter Four

Back at Furbank, Christabel had decided that talk would do her good. She said "It's so hard to know where to begin. If you saw the scenes at the pool I suppose I could work backwards, take you on a ghastly Anglo-Scottish flight with a wedding party of your Scottish Nationalists, or even take you back to a house in Half Moon Lane to which I was called to rescue Julian and first met his bloody little black-eyed Sal."

But Mozart was craftier than that. He said "My break with my wife didn't happen yesterday. But it's the significant happening. If I hadn't been through that I wouldn't have been so upset by what I saw at the pool. I wouldn't have come across to you at breakfast. So that's a beginning. There's usually a happening from which everything else stems; a kind of prime cause."

Christabel took that in, and smoked and thought very seriously. It's hard to go back to scenes that happened long before violent exchanges such as she had just lived through. But she believed in Mozart already, so she tried. She laughed nervously, and leaning her head back in the sunlight she said at last "Surprise, surprise . . . It's all my own fault. I mean I brought the whole bloody thing on my own head. Not the cancer. I refuse to take total responsibility for that. But I brought him down low..."

Mozart said "You're not telling me a tale."

It was one of those confusing moments which so frequently occurred with Mozart.

She said bewilderedly "You mean I'm lying? Or not lying? I don't follow you."

He said "I don't really believe in motives in the mirror."

"You're somewhere above my head."

"I believe I can tell whether it's your fault or not better than you can if you just give me the events. Don't distort in the looking-glass."

"Are all referees like you?"

"No. Some of them are teetotal. It's the wages they pay."

She said "But do they talk philosophy?"

"Oh yes. Glasgow's all philosophy. That's why I'm trying to keep clear of it. Just tell me the story. I'm the last great listener, here."

She said "It's not very easy to tell the story. There's so much that isn't relevant and I don't like A to Z."

"Well, give me the scene in the middle, and we'll work backwards and forwards from there."

Again, she settled back and tried to think. For quite some moments she was silent. Christabel was not so impulsive and intuitive as people believed her to be. Then she sat up on one elbow and lit yet another cigarette.

"In London," she said, "awful, greedy, unserious, shallow people like me, when they feel constrained to commit adultery, book a room for the day at one of the airport hotels."

"Great," Mozart said. He knew it was a goal.

Christabel said "My paramour was a mimic. He was rather a fat mimic who made a lot of money working the commodity market from a telephone number which was London Wall. He owned an Aston Martin motor car and a pair of enormous binoculars which he used at race meetings. He was a friend of my first husband who was a young pig. I talk in this delicious, crisp, satirical manner because this is the role I decided to play with this fat mimic from London Wall. In snobby circles to which I have been drawn like a big moth amongst the butterflies I find that people of all ages make themselves into minor characters. They put on masks and become what Mr Waugh called furniture. They adopt a certain attitude and line, even a gimmick, and play it to the point of despair. They can keep up the act everywhere except with their spouse in the home. Then they fall down, the same as everybody else, off stage.

"It is because everybody goes to one of the airport hotels that one does go to the airport hotel. I am suggesting that one secretly wishes to be caught.

"As I say, rooms can be booked for the day. The passionate romantics can eat a frozen steak with frozen peas, drink a carafe of pink liquid and retire to their pit box by two. Bathrooms are attached for wives not on the pill. There are slimming mirrors everywhere. The room is sound-proofed not only to suppress the noise of aircraft but also for the convenience of those more elderly couples who like to make excessive noise. At five o'clock a Spanish waiter, if summoned, will bring large whiskies and dyed smoked salmon sandwiches wrapped in plastic bags.

"And at five past five, on just such an afternoon, the telephone rang."

Christabel said to her paramour "It must be the waiter, again. Mimic, you'd better answer it."

"Perhaps the car," the Mimic replied, in panic, stripped all the way down to his own voice. "Or maybe they want to know when we're leaving?"

"'Departing,'" Christabel said. "That'll be it."

The telephone continued to ring. At last, very windily, the Mimic lifted the telephone and shouted in a bogus French accent: "*Allo.*"

Very evenly Julian answered "I think you should tell my wife that it is time she came home now. The children are back from school." He was speaking from their home, outside Oxford.

"Oh, right-o," the Mimic said.

Christabel had hysterics. The Mimic from the commodity market sat stock-still: petrified. He could see Christabel's backside in the mirror as she rolled on the bed, much as if someone had plunged a dagger into her lower abdomen.

"Oh Mimic," she said at last, "you're not much good at this."

She took some whisky and did the nose trick. She asked "What on earth induced you to say 'Right-o'?"

"Dunno" (in the Mimic's dustman's voice).

"What a bloody silly thing to say, anyway—'Right-o'."

"He's the only don fellow I really respect," the Mimic said sadly, and Christabel hooted with laughter again.

Then all her muscles seized up and she began to scream and scream. Her nice big, shy, wet face became very pink, then was covered by her long fair hair.

The Mimic went to the bathroom and breaking a sealed pack extracted a rough tumbler. He had once been in the R.H.A. and had required a specially large charger. He towered over the basin. He filled the tumbler with luke-warm water from the cold tap.

He paddled back to the bed nearer the window, on which she lay. Both beds were double. Both were now unmade.

He flung the water in her face.

She sat up, soaked, and said "Now what the hell did you do that for, you silly Mimic?"

He said "Because you are in hysterics, old girl."

She said "Mimic, you are not shaping up well under crisis. I did not have hysterics. And now I'm all wet. And my hair."

He said "Julian is really the only economic theoretician whom we respect, in the City, at all. Those of us who can read."

Christabel said "You mustn't fall to bits like that."

"You'd better get home," he said.

"Right-o," she replied, and laughed. "Right-o, oh, Christ."

"He sounded rather trembly on the phone," the Mimic said.

When Christabel had told her story, she felt quite exhausted. She had lain back in the sun at Furbank; she had closed her eyes as she recalled the end of the scene. She felt sober, too, and incapable of drinking more gin.

She said "Candidates are asked to judge when this scene took place, i.e. at what stage of the marriage, and to suggest the consequences of it."

She then sat up. While she had talked some players had come on the field and thirty or forty people had appeared in the grandstand. It was some sort of club trial game for the under twenty-threes.

Mozart said "We'll watch the first half. There's a kid at inside right who's meant to be very good."

Chapter Five

THE crab is an erratic eater. For days he will not cease to gnaw and squeeze and rake and suck and grow; how he grows. Then after some hours, or days, or even months he will sleep.

The room at the back of this private hotel in Lochearn-head where Julian lay had been built on to the house by a certain Matthew Matthieson, a most important member of this extraordinary wedding party with which they had all become involved on the Anglo-Scottish champagne flight. He was now their host, though Julian could not remember why or how.

The room was like a ship's cabin; a captain's cabin, and it cut right into the garden of the hotel which was built on the steep hillside. The low window was therefore at the same level as the wet, heathery rockery outside. It was a most illogical place to die.

Even if we cannot remember the incidents in our dreams, we seldom forget the tone. As Julian tried to re-construct the sequence of the last thirty-six hours he was aware that something too violent, some event too shaming and bloody, was obstructing him. There was evidence of that peculiar jumpy obscurity which comes with over-

powering guilt. He knew the worst of it had happened in
Half Moon Lane. The most he could do now was to try
to make himself remember the Anglo-Scottish flight.

The figure of Matthew came back quite easily. He was
the host of the wedding party, best man to the bridegroom
Gerry Logan. He had carried a large magnum of champagne and kept coming back to offer Julian, Christabel
and—yes, and Sally—more to drink. He was a big, aggressive man with a clean-cut face and a complexion like a
miller or a baker. He had attacked Julian for being English; had quoted bogus figures in support of an indepen-
dent Scotland; then towards the end of the journey he had
openly confessed that he was only a Scottish Nationalist
because he hated all the other parties.

Julian could remember Christabel giggling. Could remember leaning across Christabel, right across her nose, to
ask of Sally "Darling, are you all right?" The mascara
was running down Sally's cheeks. She had a bruise by her
eyebrow. The plane tilted a little. Behind her were the
green fields of Renfrew, as bright as Ireland and as sad.

Remembering her face, Julian now sat up in bed. He
called out for her. She had gone downstairs. For what?
For the wedding, of course. The thumping was the
thumping of the dancing. Somehow they had become re-
involved with Matthew and the wedding party.

He wanted only to be gentle with Sally. She was smiling
when she came back into the room. In fact she hadn't been
near the wedding. She'd been trying to ring Jacky to send
a message to Josh Reynolds. She sat down on his bed. Before he could stop it, the game, the old game, the last
game, the end game started again.

"In August we'll go away. We'll go on a boat."

He was searching for the tiniest sign of hesitation. But she didn't seem to be aware of his game. She asked "Will we get married?"

"We'll go to the Mediterranean."

"No," she said. How can a girl who is so silly be so shrewd, so very clever? "No, not in August, that would be too hot. Let's make it in September, October."

"You're very pretty."

"And only if you marry me," she said, not believing it.

He was wearing somebody else's dressing-gown. She retied the cord for him, squeezing it very tight. Maybe women like us to be wounded or ill; like us one down; feel safer like that. She walked back to the log fire.

She said with wonder "It's just like a book, specially with that wedding downstairs. Perhaps you'd better not get better. It'll get colder and colder, I don't know why. Like you say, maybe we're in Canada or Lapland or somewhere. I can keep the fire going, Matthew can chop the wood and all the snow and stuff'll come in and I'll cook you moose steaks and fried fish which he can catch through holes in the ice. I hope he traps furs, too. When it gets really bad, I shall make you a Davy Crockett nightcap. Matthew's nice. I was wrong about him. I thought he was awful and Scotch on the plane."

He reached out his arms to her. She walked quite slowly from the fire across the room to him, sat down and laid her head on his lap.

"It is longer," he said of her hair.

"I'll cut it if you want."

"No."

She said "It's going to be a miracle."

"What sort of a miracle?"

"I mean us."

His mood changed. "Why do you need a miracle?"

"Well, I mean we're going to be happy."

"But why did you say miracle?"

"Hey."

"You mean it's going to need a miracle to love a man who is sick?"

"Hey, I fancy scrambled eggs. On toast. Don't you?"

Chapter Six

At the football, Christabel at last had to admit:
"Mozart, I'm awfully sorry."

"Don't be. It's ghastly. It's not football at all."

"I'm afraid I wouldn't be able to judge that. If it were first class it still wouldn't impinge. I'd have to put a million pounds on one side before I could concentrate on the ball."

That was the nearest she got to saying that the clouds were descending. He took her by the hand and yanked her up.

On the way home, or wherever he was taking her, because she never bothered to ask, he found another diversion, quite close, in Maryhill. He said "Are you the artistic type?"

She said "No. I'm meant to be athletic."

"Oh."

She felt bad. He was trying so hard. She saw the disappointment all over those "Zs" on his face. She tried to cover. She said "How rude of me and you're being such a help. What is it?"

"It's a picture."

"Don't put me through a questionnaire."

"No, it's just a picture, really it's of a leaf or a few
leaves, nothing more. It's kept here in the Allan Ramsay
School of Drawing and it's by one of your English artists,
by a man called Lucien Freud. And it gets me. I only saw
it because I go to this college to teach them sports, they
come down to the pool. I've seen this picture. It's not
abstract. There's no tricks about it. No shit, d'you know?
It's just a few leaves, and it fascinates me because when
you've seen it you feel you've never looked at a leaf before."

"You mean it's realistic?"

"No. I mean it's true, like the opposite of other pictures
of leaves which are just that bit false ... Does that make
sense? It's become a kind of philosophy for me. I know
nothing about the man, but he's still alive, I think. And
someone once said of him 'He's got a long, unblinking
stare.' If I were an artist I'd like them to say that about
me."

They got out of the car. It was warm. She was only
going in to please him, and as she felt the sun she wondered about Julian and Sally. Thought, It's the losers that
go to the picture galleries.

But Mozart wasn't simple. It was no ordinary gallery.
The name of the place rang the vaguest bell, not that
she'd ever seen any of Ramsay's paintings: she didn't even
know who he was.

The building was on the corner of a big square, called
Ramsay Gardens. It was a most splendid Adam house,
converted to a school of drawing a hundred years before.
And why it rang a bell was that the students here had
organized a strike. It was a strike taken very unseriously by
everybody else in Scotland, mainly for the reason that the

Allan Ramsay School of Drawing, which was only vaguely attached to the university, was never considered, in itself, to be a very serious body.

The students really were asking for the simplest things. First that their syllabus be brought more in line with that of the Glasgow Tech. and, second, that there be some sort of appointments system organized for their graduates. But they asked for it at a strange time, namely shortly after the riots in Paris and Rome. They were dubbed as copyists, exhibitionists, infants and all the rest. It was probably true that they would never have struck without the European lead. But they did have a complaint. They paid money, some of them, as well as taking exams. And at the end of their course, people said "So what, you've been to the Ramsay School of Drawing? ... So now you can start in the shop."

Christabel never got to see this painting which had so impressed Mozart. For some dark reason the students were not letting visitors look round the place. In the hall, however, there were all the signs of young rebellion. Notices were stuck on statues' torsos, red flags flew beside pictures of communists and leftist philosophers. It looked very gay. There were rude cartoons about the Government and the governors, all over the place.

But on the way out Christabel was offered another diversion. Various young but obviously respectable citizens who probably worked in a shipping office, or maybe a bank, were mocking some of the students who sat under their Manifesto, selling stocks of their pamphlets and cartoons. Quite an unpleasant boyish incident was brewing up. The young business men's complaint, however, seemed to be limited to the appearance of the students: their dress and the length of their hair. They moved in to knock down the boxes and magazines and notices. The students were by no means natural pugilists. Mozart and others stepped forward to break it up. It was a passing exchange and Christabel judged that it probably happened every day. The young business men went off laughing and straightening their Rugby club ties.

She said "I don't really see what business it is of theirs."

"Right," Mozart said.

"Mind, I don't say the students too much impress me, either. I'm not sure they should strike."

"They're part of something," Mozart said. "And they're also part of Glasgow. Both those types."

"But do you think that kind of strike is of any value?"

"It has involved your interest," he replied.

Mind, if you've never been to Glasgow, you should make your first trip in wintertime when the neon lights burn all day in the windows of the rows and rows of little, economically impossible shops. The proprietors have to light up because the sky comes out of the docks and rests on the tenement roofs, like a blanket over the pain.

But even in the sunshine, there are some breathtakingly nasty vistas. The buses go up and down hills very fast; they nudged Mozart's old Ford into the gutter as he showed the city to Christabel, with pride.

He said "If you notice that some of the new buildings look like fortresses you shouldn't blame the architects. They first put in glass where the local authorities have since been obliged to build in bricks. We are a violent race."

And on the walls of some of the old buildings Christabel was shown the evidence of real local power. This did not consist of old posters saying I.L.P. or S.N.P. or Ewing or Vote Communist, why not?—*Christ died for you.* Chalked beside, below and over these notices were the names of local gangsters, and some of the gangs are eighty or ninety strong. Written large: "Handy Barr Rule"—him and his weirdly nicknamed partners in fear; Wee Tam and Bike Cheyne and Pluto-with-a-knife.

Mozart stopped the car by a disused Congregational church hall the other side of Gallowgate to show his guest a significant message chalked up in a childish hand. It read, very wee: This is Goblin Land.

"There's Glasgow true," Mozart said, and he seemed to know. It turned out that he lived in premises above a shop he called his own, though it was mortgaged to the hilt. It was next door to a doctor's surgery which looked like a grocers', with "Dr J. Brodie & Dr K. Forsythe" marked in big, bold letters above the window and door. They were known locally as Dr Jekyll and Dr Jekyll. "We are a macabre people."

The street was familiar to Celtic supporters, it being close to their ground, the wrong side of Glasgow Green; a district which is neither Irish as popularly imagined, nor Jewish, nor Jamaican, but sheer Glasgow. Here on the walls by pissy wynds and murderous passageways there were absent landlords' agents' notices about Burst Pipes. These were the only indication of the hand of authority. Scored up beside the one next to Mozart's shop was a smudged Glaswegian tragedy: "Maureen loves Willum true."

The host double locked his Ford and set the patent

burglar alarm, under the bonnet. "We are not an honest people."

She said "Mozart, is yours supposed to be any particular kind of shop, or is it just a general trading agency? From the window, it's impossible to tell."

Mozart seemed to find it difficult to explain. He said "You'd think the youth here would buy things like footballs and punchballs or even isometric dumb-bells. That's what I thought. But they buy rubber balls if they buy any at all and most of them are quite happy with a tin can. And if you try and sell camping equipment the only turnover is in the flick-knife department. I grew to think those sales were touching anti-social. Then a salesman caught me once when I was paralytic drunk, which I was for a year or two after my wife went, and I bought two dozen lacrosse sticks from him. Then I got a job-lot of mouth-organs and I went into music with terrible new drums and some guitars they make in Falkirk. It's more of a hobby really, my shop. I consider it wrong that I shouldn't be able to live decently as a full-time referee."

Upstairs, the flat was unbelievably chaotic.

Mozart said "I told you I broke up the furniture."

"You didn't say you never washed the plates."

"No, I didn't."

In one corner there was a big surgical bench or bed on which Mozart manipulated athletes.

"But not for pleasure," he said. "Illegally for money, if they twist something. The girls who are kind enough to oblige me get taken to the bedroom next door."

"I see," Christabel said.

He found the teapot, at last, and there were some tea

bags on the window-sill. The kettle stopped whistling as he asked "You are full of guilt?"

"Yes."

"You are so full of guilt that you actually persuade yourself that you reduced your husband's resistance to such an extent that he contracted this horrible disease."

"Yes."

"The candidate wants to know more about Julian's first operation, like where did you say it was?"

"The truth about smoking. The lungs. He was operated on at the Radcliffe."

"How long ago was that?"

"Eighteen months ago. A little more."

"So you and the Mimic were surprised in the airport hotel a little before that, say two years ago?"

"Wrong," she said.

"Ah."

She told him "The Mimic happened three months *after* the first operation. Julian had returned home, by then, and was walking about the house. He had not begun to work again but he was reading. He was doing some research."

"On what?"

"On nap."

"Nap? Racing news?"

"Yes. He was following the racing results. He's really very ingenious, my Julian. He made a little study which proved that the tipsters on horse racing know more, considerably more than all the financial editors, columnists and investment advisers who write about stocks and shares."

"Proving?"

"Well, he got rather discouraged by that. In the end he began to think it only proved that horse racing was as dishonest as everybody always thought it was. So he rather back tracked. Anyway, about then he was also ingenious enough to ring up that ass of mine who registered under his own name at the airport hotel."

"And the consequence?"

"You are the candidate. It's a good game. The only way of forgetting people you love desperately seems to be to talk of them as they were. I'm finding that out for the first time. Even when they jilt you, they cannot take away from you the memory—no, more, the *fact* of their once having been the lovers they were... The candidate is asked to describe the scene when the adulteress got home."

Mozart put two big teaspoonfuls of sugar in her tea, as he settled to play the game. She yelled too late. He therefore put a couple of measures of whisky in to take away the taste.

Noticing the bottles in the cardboard box, she said "You don't do yourself too badly."

He said "My bankruptcy is a standard to which one day many referees throughout the world will rally. It is a very serious kind of bankruptcy. It's bankruptcy with malice aforethought. The more scandalous my debts can become, the greater will be my glory and the subsequent reforms. Think of these bottles not as Black and White, but as a fine athletic cause."

She had settled on an armchair with a broken leg, curling up her feet to keep them out of the dirty plates. He lay on the surgical bench, flat on his back. He removed his spectacles.

He said "It's not at all an easy one for the candidate . . .

Unlike myself in similar circumstances your husband has blown the fact that he knows you've been unfaithful. He rang the airport hotel. It would seem to lead to a very unpleasant and recurring series of rows in the home, such as we see in adulterous TV plays, every second night. If we were heading for bad 'Virginia Woolf' material, however, you wouldn't set the question, therefore there was no row?"

"Right."

"But he was at home?"

"Yes."

"In bed?"

"No."

"Working?"

"No."

He said "I'm getting cold. You'll have to play the scene."

Again she thought for a long time before she spoke. She smoked half a cigarette.

She said at last "I will tell you what happened, exactly, in a minute. But at the time I did not understand what had happened. Not at all. Really it's only now after that awful shouting match which you witnessed at the pool, yesterday—it's only now that I see what really happened.

"Therefore you must come back one step with me, if the scene of my return from the airport is to make any real sense.

"When they took out this tumour on the lung the surgeon told both Julian and myself the same story. He was amazed by the size of the growth. He pretended he could not explain it. He seemed to imply that it might not after all be malignant, meaning deadly. But he didn't quite say as much. He said the lab boys were at work. Meantime, however, he said he wanted to give Julian some deep-ray treatment in order to clean up any odds and ends left behind—'just for safety's sake'. Obviously this preyed on my mind and I had to know. I kept visiting the Pathology department and being fobbed off: 'Nothing positive on the test', 'We'll be in touch'. All that.

"Meantime Julian came home. The deep-ray treatment seemed to depress him less than most people. He was niggly a little, and unapproachable in a strange, sad way. He was like an only child in the house. You know how they have complicated toys or hobbies and they drift away to their own room to play with their chemistry set or whatever. He didn't want to see other people very much. Kept telling me to go out and enjoy myself. He ate very lightly and would only drink champagne. I went back to Pathology. They then started giving me the story that the cells were unstable and therefore the specimen no longer significant. They kept giving me false hope. So at last I managed to get an interview with the great doctor scientist in charge, who turned out to be about fourteen with hair like a mouse. He was very alarmed by my direct question. He too refused to say that it was cancer; insisted that he didn't know, then said that if the growth was malignant it still was by no means fatal. If a year or two went by and there were no secondaries then there was nothing to worry about.

"You find you come away from all these interviews feeling happier but not absolutely satisfied. You find yourself going back to the surgeon and asking him exactly the same questions all over again.

"Julian didn't ask any questions. Not once he was out of the hospital. That was the most extraordinary thing. He seemed quite ready to forget about the lab tests. He simply lost interest in them. I think the deep-ray treatment following the operation made him dread hospitals so much that he just blotted all that out of his mind. In hospital he had cross-examined the doctors several times but after that he never raised the question at all. He lived from day to day. He lived separately from us all. He slept in a separate room.

"I only arrived at that bloody airport hotel because I have such a social conscience. I got drunk at a military party actually in St James's Palace, or drunk enough to accept an invitation for lunch at the airport the next day. There was talk of going over to some race-meeting in France, not that I believed that. Next day, I didn't have this Mimic's phone number so I couldn't cancel, that way. I made about five excuses to Julian, not one, for being out that afternoon, then drove like mad to the airport hotel. After the first few moments with this Barrington-Scrumptious I began to think it would be lamentable and wet of me to have a rendezvous like this, eat a bad lunch, then go home undone. So if anything, I rather forced the pace. Said 'If we're going to do it, let's get on with it.'"

She had finished her explanation. She said "The candidate now has a second chance. What was the consequence of the husband's telephone call to the airport hotel?"

The candidate poured himself more tea, which was now lukewarm and black. He still sat on the surgical bench.

"I know the eventual consequence. You've told us that. He took a job in London, in the Cabinet Office."

"Right."

"Which would be better paid?"

"Much, much better paid. I mean really very well paid."

The candidate lit a cigarette. He wanted to get it right in one.

He asked "Am I allowed to put a few more questions before plumping for a conclusion?"

"Yes."

He said "There's one thing confusing me. Not merely the champagne, but the talk of St James's, the buzzing up to London, even the reference to the only child and the separate bedroom—all these things add up to a picture of university life which doesn't fit with paying guests and penniless dons."

"Very good."

"What exactly was this party at St James's?"

"When they're guarding what they call Buck House the officers have a special little mess in St James's Palace and there they give tiny dinner-parties: at which, be it added, the food is typically male and pretentious. A girl friend of mine was the lover of the Company Commander. The Mimic and I were the other guests."

"This was the kind of party you did not want to miss?"

Christabel laughed. "You are so right. And you're absolutely on the ball. Dons still become dons in the same way as before. They have to be as brilliant, if not more so because the competition is even stiffer. But for some time now, really since the war, or since TV and Industry started spending money in research and all that, lots of dons at Oxford have not been nearly so penniless as they like to make out. Historians have become national celebrities. All the scientists are potential consultants. The same goes for philosophers and economists. Therefore a certain new, altogether more racy group of dons with houses outside Oxford, has tended to grow up. And as they are rather attractive men, county ladies have got involved. The sensible dons married ladies with money. They were wise to, because it is one thing to be richer than the lecturer in the room below and quite another to be able to keep up with the kind of people who live in Oxfordshire, Berkshire, Gloucestershire and London. Julian did not marry money. He married me. I had been used to living alongside people with money and of course I wanted the right kind of house, dinner party and all that. I don't mean social climbing. I just mean fun. And of course I then started to make Julian live the kind of life which wasn't the one he set out to live. In other words my debts, my constant compulsion to spend twenty-two shillings in the pound gradually corrupted his scholarship. That's my guilt. That's where we came in. That's why I blame myself."

She left it there, and Mozart said "If what I think happened happened, this is indeed a very rare case. It's a play called 'Adultery Rewarded', only it's a comedy."

She answered "I think you are going to get it right, but it was only comic so far."

"Here goes," Mozart said . . . "I can't give you the detail of the scene but here's the principle: when Julian discovered that you had been unfaithful to him it gave him a new lease of life because he did not believe that you would do such a thing to a dying man."

"Mozart, I am sure you are an excellent referee."

"I'm right?"

"Yes. Absolutely. Though I didn't twig at the time. Actually, I got a break of luck. The Mimic insisted on following me the whole way home. Our house is more or less in the middle of a village and he parked in the street outside because I didn't want him to come in. I breezed in, absolutely shaking in my shoes because Julian—as you saw at the pool—has got the most fearful temper when it's roused, which isn't often. His mother happened to have dropped by. She follows the horses, so the two of them were deep in a discussion about nap and all that. This third party gave us both the out. We didn't have to raise the subject and we didn't have to *not* raise it too obviously. In other words there was something to talk about . . . Champagne all round as you can guess . . . About an hour later Julian looked out of the hall window and said 'Chris, you'd better tell that ass in the Bentley to go away or he'll cause a traffic accident.' I was then quite brave. I rushed up to him and kissed him on both cheeks and he must have felt me trembling like a leaf. Then I opened the window and shouted to Barrington-Bum to buzz off. A sunny, rainy evening. We have ivy on our wall . . . Next day Julian went into college. Within three weeks he accepted the job at the Cabinet Office which meant we could pay off most of the debts. The hospital was B.U.P.A., thank God. He moved back into my room. I felt everything was going to be all right, though I sometimes wondered if he really loved me. I guessed he did. He's very wise and mature in the way the best dons can be, and therefore is capable of controlling the ego better than most. Is capable of forgiving a girl. You're looking doubtful. You don't think he loved me?"

"No," Mozart said. "That's not what I'm thinking."

He smiled very kindly. "I'm thinking I'm the loser here. You're going to get your husband back."

"Am I? How? When?" At this moment she still seemed to want him back, desperately. "There isn't much time, you know."

Chapter Seven

WHEN Jacky had returned from her Export-Import Arab to Half Moon Lane, Sid and Simon said that the phone had been ringing for her all day. And at once it rang again.

Sally, still at Lochearnhead, was speaking from a callbox under the stairs. She chain-smoked as she talked. Always, on the phone, she settled down for a long chat. She said "You sound quite clear. You sound like next door."

"Yes, it is a good line."

"You don't sound too pleased to hear me."

"Well," Jacky said.

"Well what?"

"Well you said how you'd ring last night. I stayed in, specially. Josh was on. And again breakfast time. And that Shelley. And your mother. And I didn't know what I have to say."

"Say as I was swimming in Glasgow."

"Did you win anything?"

"If you'd seen the state I was in by the time the race began you'd ask if I sunk. No I did not win. I was fourth. Even that cow from Blackpool beat me. She'd the nerve to come up afterwards and ask me if it was the wrong time of the month. I'm finished with competitive sports, I am."

"She didn't really?"

"She did. I said 'No, as a matter of fact I'd had a busy evening, drunk half a bottle of vodka, smoked forty cigarettes, been laid by a big space-walker, then beaten half to death and raped by the man I love, who brought his wife for breakfast . . .' 'Oh yes?' the little cow said."

"Sal, did I hear you right?"

"Yes you did. I love him. Julian, I mean."

"Sal, last week, it was all fixed. I mean your mum's asking if Sunday's on for her to meet Josh. She's talking about where the wedding is, here or Pasadena. She doesn't half grasp the details, your mum. She knows all about Pasadena, says how in its way it's better than Beverly Hills."

"Well, she's just got to put it out of her mind again. I'm with Julian and Christabel's not."

"What made you switch, then?"

"I've been reading my diary."

"Oh Sal."

"Not only that. I mean reading it, and remembering all those times and, I don't know, I just fell in love with him again, that's all."

"What are you going to say to Josh?"

"I'm not. You are."

"Oh no, I'm not."

"I'm going to write him."

"'Dear John.'"

"Well 'Dear Josh'."

"Haven't you heard of 'Dear John'? They're the letters men in the Forces used to get from their wives when they'd gone off with the commercial traveller or whoever. What made you change your mind?"

She didn't believe the diary story. It is extraordinary, really, how understatement is part and parcel of all English exchange. Two French girls would be talking about which man was Sal's *réalité*, by now.

Jacky said, "After what he did to you two nights ago—"

"I know. It's funny, in'it?"

"Maybe I'll tell Josh to get a belt and put you over his knee."

"Ooooh."

"Sally, you sure? I mean Josh loves you too. Not the same maybe, but more normal. And he's not married. I don't think that Christabel'll let Julian go easy."

"That's all over."

"How over?"

"Well, there was a scene at the pool. Before I even had time to get my clothes on, just at the end, when the judge is reading out the time and result of the free-style Julian comes down to say well-tried or whatever you do tell the loser. Then Christabel comes down too. I think she's scared he'll fall in the pool. You know how he gets. Then all of a sudden he was absolutely furious with her for taking his elbow when he slipped. He couldn't have staged it better. There's all the competitors and judges round about and there must have been a hundred and twenty spectators. Suddenly he's waving his arms, yelling and shouting at her, and one of the judges, the young one, he ushers us all out and tells me to go downstairs and change. Julian's still screaming and yelling how she's a nanny and trying to kill him and all sorts. It was horrible, really."

"Sounds awful. I mean, is he all right in the head?"

"Julian? No. He never was."

"But was it his bawling out Christabel makes you change your mind?"

"I always did say I'd marry him if he wanted to leave her. So now he's left her."

"But that's not forever, a row like that."

"I wouldn't say that. To tell you the truth he said things to her I'd never come up from, myself. Never. I don't know if she's got my pride. Then I spoke to her for a moment before we went off."

"What did she say?"

"Oh, nothing, really. She tried to frighten me off, I think."

Nobody knew when Sally was lying except her sister Shelley. But Jacky wasn't quite satisfied.

She said "She must have said something."

Sally said "I don't remember what she said."

But that was a downright lie. She also remembered very well what she had replied when Christabel told her "He has only a few weeks left." She replied "Not with me, he hasn't." She was proud of that.

It was true that she had been beaten up and more or less raped by the man she loved. That was the scene which obstructed Julian's recollection. After the electrical engineer had switched off Sportsview and retired upstairs, Sally had told Julian, untruthfully, that the cushions from the settee had been put on the floor by Josh Reynolds, not by Jacky's Bill. The lie alone should have revealed to her whom she really loved. But the vodka was by then empty and Julian believed her story. Perhaps it was that they both wanted to believe her story. She'd asked for violence. It was just that she misjudged how much he had to give. At the end she was naked and bruised and bleeding and moaning. Then one of the boys came in and struck Julian: hit him until he passed out.

Chapter Eight

Mozart and Christabel went from his digs to the Central Hotel, where she had told Julian she would stay for twenty-four hours, before returning south. Where he and Sally were now, she had no idea. They had vanished, together, and there was still no message from them.

She should have gone home, there and then, but she could not face the loneliness.

She asked Mozart "Do you mind if I cling? Just for a little longer?"

"I wouldn't let you go."

"You don't think I'd do anything stupid?"

"Kill yourself?"

"That kind of thing."

"No, you won't do that."

"I wouldn't put it past me."

She kept to gin and tonic but he now started on beers with whisky chasers. He had an enormous capacity. He took her to big, horrible pubs, not hotel bars.

She said "You must be the kindest person I've ever met."

He said "No, I'm just nosy."

She said "I've smoked forty-four cigarettes already today."

He said "These games. This business of him always saying where we'll go next Christmas and wanting to apply for posts in India, just in order to test your re-action—"

She nodded. "They've been getting worse. I mean, since he came back from hospital he plays them all the time, not only with me but with any visitor. More particularly with visitors because they're more likely to give something away."

"But do they know he's dying?"

"I don't tell them."

"They guess?"

She said "People like the very sick to die. We all push them over in the end."

Mozart was about to apply some of the old bromides: "While there's life," that kind of thing. But he left them unsaid.

He said "From what you've said the games seem to be far from direct. He's gone on about sickness: about it being hard for you, about 'in sickness and in health' being a tough clause?" She nodded. He said "Also about the lack of sex?"

"Yes."

"But he's never come right out and said 'So I'm dying, woman, why don't you stop trying to kid me?'"

"Never. Well . . ."

"Well?"

"Well, once, the very nearest he got to it was—actually he was in less pain than usual, it was one of the better mornings. We've got a dog. A big labrador, I'd sent it into the bedroom with the newspapers. He never likes the dog near him when he's in bad pain. The dog's a good sign. One sunny day, like that, he said to me 'All fatal illnesses are only marginal examples of an ageing process common to us all.'"

"Just out of the blue, he said that?"

"More or less. I was just walking about the room, putting some flowers in the vases, I think ... I didn't turn back to him. It wasn't a bad moment and yet it's a moment that has stuck."

Mozart said "The candidate is asked to explain why."

She practically disappeared in her own smoke screen before emerging at last to say: "I can't pin this down. I'll circle twice, then if you haven't got the answer you can ask me more specific questions. Okay?"

"The examiner has all night before him."

"Right. I'm going to talk about morals, religion, manners and Julian." She suddenly burst out laughing. She said "Just a tiny dissertation."

"Julian's father was an absolute poppet."

Mozart said "Watch that language."

She continued: "No, but he was. I'm sorry. It describes him. He was a tiny man, very gentle and sensitive and very Christian. He was a canon, but all the time I knew him he had retired to this minute church and parish in the Cotswolds. He was there for the last twenty years of his life. He married when he was about forty-five. There were two sons, the first one was killed in the war. This may have brought the couple even more firmly together. But whatever the reasons, it was a perfect marriage. She had the real intelligence. She was bigger than him. She was the daughter of one of those Cambridge families, Pryor or Darwin, or Trevelyan, half of them are mixed up. She was quite pretty and also a firm Christian. She was extremely well-read and though he was alone, Julian truly had the most extraordinary childhood, in quite idyllic surroundings. That's by the way. The point I am making is that the parents had faith. And discipline. A great deal of discipline. They lived perfectly within a small income, they were extremely temperate, they took immense trouble over acquaintances and never failed to take an interest in the young. Communists, atheists, even Presbyterians were treated alike. When one thinks that they lived this life in England so short a time ago, frankly, it makes you want to weep. They really did know what love was about. They were good. And the word good is the last and only word which makes me cry."

Recovering, and it was necessary to her to recover, she went on: "From this stable you would expect a tearaway and possibly the elder son was going that way, I don't know. Not so Julian. Mainly because he has all his mother's brains. But he did separate in one way which hurt all three terribly. He simply was incapable of faith. When he was at home he would go to church, and behave as if nothing had happened within him. This was not hypocrisy, but a question of manners. The old people curiously enough abhorred religious discussion. Their Christianity rested absolutely on faith, not on reason. It was a gift. They were sad to see that their son was not fortunate enough to have this gift, and he in turn felt bad about their sadness. It is difficult to talk of these subtle ties between three good people, because the secret about Julian, the extraordinary secret is that he is also good. His sickness

is evil. I am absolutely sure of this. In the same way that
he mentions a future trip to India to test me, to play his
games, he also very much wants to go to India or one of
the underdeveloped countries because he believes that his
knowledge can help people there.

"It is difficult to describe the good, without bringing on
the milk and water but the iron is also there. It is the discipline. But something terrible happened, maybe not within
himself but in the world. The discipline of his parents was
a joyful thing because it led to glory. It was an optimistic
discipline. It had purpose. Julian talked of all this to me,
believe it or not, also in idyllic circumstances. In fact in a
punt, in the sun, on the Isis. He was a very, very serious
lover when I came along and fucked up his whole way of
life."

Again she had to recover to say: "He was also a roman-
tic lover. He cut off a lock of my hair. I believe he carries
it in his wallet, still.

"Julian has described to me his whole moral philosophy
of life as the discipline of impossibility. It is not so complicated, and if you look around at intelligent Englishmen
it is not at all uncommon. It is not a hopeless philosophy.
He doesn't say 'There's no point, forget it, if there's a God
he must be malevolent'; he is not as continental as that.
But it is a pessimistic outlook. It is a kind of controlled
pessimism. He does not see joy ahead. He does not believe
that passion will not pall. He does not expect that money
will bring happiness. He does not believe that the toys will
never break. He does not sleep with somebody else's wife
because he foresees the pain ahead. Now Julian's an anti-
theory man. He does not believe that any theory will provide all the answers. Therefore he wouldn't go so far as

to say that he is the arch example of the Anglican hangover. He lives his life more or less within the discipline of his parents, more or less within the same code, and not only does he not experience the joy they knew, he doesn't expect to experience it. He has passed some of this pessimism on to my children, I don't know how. They don't answer 'Yes' to the world ... I say Anglican. Perhaps I put too much emphasis on the church, too little on England itself. I believe that the last people to think along Julian's lines were probably the prosperous Romans in Britain. Without faith or too much ambition they to some extent disciplined themselves toward the cultivation of their gardens. Again, that's my suggestion, not Julian's. He'd never be so rash.

"The examiner must begin to wonder if I have forgotten the question. But I haven't.

"When Julian said to me 'All fatal illnesses are only marginal examples of an ageing process common to us all', he put in one sentence this whole stoic, depressing English philosophy. And the fact that he said that out loud, at this point was a signal to me, outside the games. When his father was dying he told Julian's mother 'We have all eternity before us.' Those were almost his last words. Julian was saying the same to me. In a moment out of pain he was offering me all the comfort he has to offer, namely 'We're not really much worse off than anybody else.' But he doesn't believe in death-bed scenes, or in lovers' last exchanges. Not with me at any rate, and I take that as a mark of respect. He simply doesn't believe in the truth of the phrases we might exchange. That's the whole logical-positive bit which is part and parcel of all economists. The semantics. The distrust of ideas in themselves. The feeling

that there is a hitch in every projection, even in any state-
ment of love and gratitude itself.

"That's about as far as I can go. And that remark of
his was made about three weeks ago. Thereafter he hasn't
said so much to me. He hasn't really played the games
with me. Then, hell, all of a sudden one day when I'm in
Oxford taking the kids to some rich man's pool he ups
and outs. A taxi to Didcot, catches the afternoon train to
London when he can hardly stand on his own two feet
and the next time I met him, well . . . Well, that was at
her dump in Half Moon Lane."

Mozart stayed quiet for a moment. There was something about her, a tiny shakiness in her voice which made
him sure that she was about to face the worst scenes, any
moment now.

She said "He was like a different man there. I can only
think that it's pathological. That the bloody disease literally touches the brain."

"I don't think you quite believe that."

"Right," she said. Then very bravely she admitted "I
just want to believe it. I know."

She was trembling badly.

Mozart said "Now, steady."

"I do so want to believe it. That it isn't really him doing
all this."

"Steady."

She didn't cry. She smoked and smoked.

But she couldn't leave the bone alone. Mozart understood that. They went back to one of the big lounges
upstairs at the Central Hotel, an anonymous kind of place
with a hundred not quite leather chairs. There were some

business men at the other end of the room drinking beers, but they were half a mile out of earshot.

Mozart said "I think I know what happened."

"Speak."

Mozart shook his head. "I'll need to ask some questions, I'll need to get some of the facts you half swallowed all day. But I'm building to some kind of conclusion. Are you sure you want to talk now?"

"I'm sure of nothing."

"I'll tell you of my sexual experiences instead, if you want," he said dolefully; "there's tragedy there."

She smiled. She said "I don't know what I would have done if I hadn't met you."

"But you did meet me."

"Thank God."

"Which puts a crack straight through the middle of your neo-Anglican pessimism."

"Believe me, it's not mine."

"Do you want my sexual orgies?"

"I'm sorry ... I can't really get my mind beyond Julian."

In the end she seemed to enjoy answering the questions. If she hadn't, Mozart would have left it for another day. He put each question carefully and seriously. He asked, first:

Had you ever heard of Half Moon Lane before? Never. Let's face it. I'm one of those who thinks South London is a nasty maze that lies between the Thames and the car ferry at Lydd. Maybe I paint myself too badly. I suppose I'd been to Dulwich which is just up the road.

Did you ever suspect in the year between the illnesses that he was having an affair? Of course I didn't suspect. You don't suspect somebody you love and somebody who has forgiven you. It's really like saying do you suspect your father of sleeping soixante-neuf with your mother. You don't walk about the place thinking that kind of thing, unless you're very sick. I always think wives who find out, then further complain because everybody except themselves must have known, are on the wrong track. It's a nice normal thing to be the last to know. But of course you're bound to replay some of the scenes, even love scenes that occurred simultaneously. After his recovery, Julian became a very active lover again. That galls me a bit. I like bed.

Did he ever mention Sally? Not once.

So when he rang you up from Half Moon Lane you didn't expect to find him with a girl? You've got that wrong. He didn't ring me up. A young man by the name of Simon rang me up. And when I got there, after having been half way round Kennington, Brixton, Bromley and God knows where, I found a house full of people.

Detail? On the phone Simon said that they had picked up my husband on the street and hadn't wanted to ring the police. They thought he was an alcoholic. Actually, Simon, Sid and what's her name, the girl friend, had genuinely decided that he was an alcoholic. I can't think that our Miss Cohen did, because she must have known him better than that. When I arrived at the door, Simon, who was a very nice young man with big ears, said that Julian had come round and was in the parlour.

Was it a messy kind of house? These things are relative,

Mozart dear. Relative to your pad it was a well-organized and delightful semi-detached villa in a nice part of town. Relative to mine it was... What was it?... It was just a digs. The kind of house that is run quite legitimately by a small landlord as a source of income. Everything was cheap, nothing was disgusting. It smelt of bodies, but young bodies, not birdseed and old women. But it was also something of a mad house.

Describe the madness. It centred round Miss Cohen. I actually first saw her in that strange way one can see someone through the crack of a door. I mean by the hinge. The door was half open but I was standing just inside the hall, brushing some mud off my feet on the mat and I caught a glimpse of her. I looked up, I guess, because I heard a girl rampaging. Completely out of control. She was shouting at another rather placid, short girl. She was pulling out drawers and sweeping the shelf of a cupboard on to the floor. Two seconds later, she bolted out of that room and arrived in the hall. She was very surprised to find me there and stopped in her tracks, a moment which I then did not realize would stick in my brain for the rest of my life, but it will. I have to be very fair. Before I twigged who and what she was, and I didn't find out until much later, I thought "My God, what an attractive child". Child's the word. Her cheeks were pink with rage. Her eyes jet black, sort of Malayan black. Her hair the same. She was in stocking soles. A by no means cheap camel coloured mini skirt and a dark shirt with clean white collar and cuffs. Then she turned away and ran off. As she did so she put her hand on the bobble at the bottom of the bannisters, so that she wheeled around into the back of the house even faster. At about the same moment two young men in duffle coats came thundering downstairs. They were carrying students' wallets with zips. They yelled "Sorry", "Bye", and thundered past me into the street. They were evidently late for their bus. Simon called for this other girl. Her name was Jacky. She emerged. Simon said "This is Julian's wife." "Oh," Jacky said, "*Ciao*". She was quite punch drunk. She was in a transparent negligée and pyjamas. She said, "If you like to come this way, Mrs... er... a-mm..."

Still you didn't suspect that Julian had been to this house before? That's rather like saying "Did the passengers suspect the wind was coming from the north quarter when they leapt off the *Titanic*?" I mean I'd lost a husband, been rung up, got lost myself, found the house and all I've described must have taken less than a minute.

Was Julian surprised to see you? Not in the least, it would seem. He was looking pretty awful and crumpled sitting on the arm of a chair amongst all the debris that Miss Cohen had flung about the place. He said "Hello darling, it appears that Miss Cohen has lost her swimming suit."

Jacky said "Not to worry. These drawers needed going over anyway." She then knelt down and started to shove the stuff back in the drawers and shelves.

Really, it was a most extraordinary scene. All this at eight o'clock in the morning. I kissed Julian on the cheek and because I didn't want to play nanny or worried mother, I said, kind of idiotically, "Has she only got one bathing costume?"

"Not her," Jacky said, "she's got four but she's only got one lucky one she says."

"Miss Cohen is a swimming champion," Julian explained, and I gave him a cigarette.

At which point yet another young man, one Sid, bounded into the room.

Julian said, in his careful way, "Sidney plays Rugby football for Blackheath."

Sid was slapping the door. He grinned, nodded hullo to me and then said to Julian, "I can get you Anglo-Scottish, first class," a somewhat memorable reservation. He asked "How many d'you want, then?"

"Well," Julian said. "Now that Christabel's arrived I think we'd better have three places ... Sidney has a pull with Anglo-Scottish."

"Where are we going?"

"Glasgow. Miss Cohen is swimming in the National—"

"No," Jacky said, "it's not National. It's just the Jansen Cup. Them and the *Mail*, I think."

Jacky flatly refused to go through and speak to Sally, while she was in that kind of mood. So Julian told Christabel to go, instead.

Christabel found the door to the bedroom and kitchen closed. She knocked, and knocked again. There was still no reply so she entered. The curtain was closed but it was unlined and light also burst through the chinks. The far bed, Jacky's, was most noticeably unmade. The mattress was half on the floor. The contents of the wardrobe (which half filled the room) and every drawer were flung all over the floor. Sally's stockinged feet were revealed at the end of her bed. Otherwise she was completely covered, head as well, by the yellow eiderdown. The bed had not been slept in. She was lying face downwards on the red counterpane.

Christabel said "What colour is the lucky one?" She started rummaging about the floor.

"Not this orange one?" But as soon as she looked at it she could see that it would not be used in competition swimming.

The form on the bed did not move.

Christabel took a dressing-gown, two coats and three dresses covered in polythene bags off a single hook on the back of the kitchen door. It had occurred to her that a costume might have been taken in there to be dried. She found one, beneath.

She stepped back into the bedroom. She said, "Would it be navy blue with white piping?"

Very slowly a hand pulled the quilt back. Sally turned and smiled.

"Wherever was it?"

Christabel showed her. She said, "Sidney's booked an Anglo-Scottish flight."

"I don't want to go," Sally said and lay down again.

Christabel said "I know the feeling."

"You don't swim?"

"No. I used to ski."

"You're not old."

"I still ski. I don't race any more, thank God. It was always a ghastly cloudy day the morning of a big race. I used to hang on to the bedclothes—"

"Yes. That's it."

"I just wanted to be forgotten."

"Yes, that's it exactly. Pretend how you've forgotten the day. Ring up later, say 'Oh dear, I am sorry.'"

"Do you need a towel?"

"Not the green one."

Christabel smiled.

"No, it matters to me that kind of thing," Sally said.

"I know. Which is the towel?"

"Really, I don't think I will go. I had hardly any sleep. I've been smoking all week."

Christabel had picked out the only dark blue towel amongst the debris on the floor.

"This one?"

"How did you know? What time is it?"

"We'll make the plane if you rush. We've got an hour and fifteen minutes."

"Until take-off? Cripes."

Sally dashed into the bathroom. She washed in the kitchen sink with a tartan cloth. She said "I'll bet that Jacky's been using this on the plates. And the pots." She said "First race isn't until two, is it, I don't know. There's heats in the morning, maybe. You got to be there for heats even if you're on a bye."

She scrubbed her face very hard and without any make-up, Christabel guessed, she was maybe sixteen at most.

Sally asked "Is skiing dangerous?"

"Yes."

"D'you have to train?"

"You should do."

"I know what you mean. Don't I. I wouldn't go, you know, not if you hadn't found the navy blue."

"You'll win."

"No, don't say that."

"Anyhow, let's get there first."

"You're not coming?"

"I really don't know. Julian seemed to think so."

Sally was changing out of her skirt. Her mind seemed

to be far away. Christabel said she'd wait next door. As she left the room the phone rang, on the landing.

Mozart was a hound dog. He kept snuffling back to the main scent. He said "Fine, I think I've got the correct impression of chaos and confusion in Half Moon Lane, but I'm a devil for a thesis and you're not helping me to it, for a moment. The area I'm trying to reach is the space between you and Julian at this point. By the time we're in Glasgow the whole thing's out in the open, or damned near. At least he's calling Sally 'darling' and treating you icily. Right?"

"So right. That's what he was doing on the plane, too, when we weren't drinking toasts for Mr Gerry Logan, the lugubrious groom."

"But when you're still back in the Half Moon Lane bedroom looking for blue bathing-suits and talking about Down Hill Only and all that, two girlish competitors together, you have no idea whatsoever that she's your rival?"

"Not the foggiest idea. Or had I? I was rather patronizing to her. I didn't *consciously* suspect."

"So when Sally goes up to take the phone, still half dressed, and you return to the front parlour, does something dawn on you then?"

"No."

"Weren't you a bit slow, here?"

"I don't think so. Julian was crafty about this point. And here we're back to Julian-as-Julian-was and Julian-as-now. In conference in the Cabinet or All Souls or wherever, he must always have played with skill, I suppose, or older men wouldn't have turned up at home so often and asked his advice. Maybe that part of his brain was now pitched against mine, but I'm sure his manner was different, too. I'd never seen him behave in quite the way he then behaved. Can I take a very small loop?"

"Permission granted."

People say "In vino veritas". I don't believe in that at all. All sorts of nice old dons I know become excessively cruel and horrid when they're drunk and I've never seen evidence to support the idea that they are, *au fond*, horrid men. For them, and especially the older they get, they simply seem to exercise all their hostilities and complexes when they're drunk. They take the bad dog out of the kennel for an airing, but it's only one dog in the pack and it doesn't represent the whole spirit of the pack. Whether through sheer exhaustion, pain or drugs or booze or all of these things, I don't know—Julian now became rather crafty. He played a very cynical kind of rôle as if Jacky and Miss Cohen and all the others were simply specimens who diverted him. He spoke to me quite audibly, but totally ignoring Jacky's presence.

He said "Isn't this a splendid scene? You didn't believe all this stuff about the swim suit?"

"Yes I did. I found her navy blue one. She's all right. She's going to Glasgow."

He said "That's all irrelevant. The truth is that she's become engaged to somebody she doesn't love."

From the floor, or almost from the depths of the cupboard, Jacky said "That's not fair. She told me how she'd kill herself if anything happened to Josh."

Julian chuckled at that. "We all love Jacky very much," he said.

But Jacky looked quite annoyed with him. "That's what she told me."

Julian was being very destructive. His laughter was cynical and horrible. He seemed to be bent on bringing this house down on his head. I had the feeling that he had been behaving in this way all night. I sensed that they were all a little afraid of him and that's why they had rung me up. Of course I wondered vaguely how the hell he had got there in the first place, but parties do just suddenly happen and there was all the evidence around, what with dirty glasses, plates, ashtrays.

At about that point, however, I began to suspect that much more had passed in the house than the arrival and subsequent relapse into a coma of a very sick man. There was the strangest atmosphere. The thought had got no further when Sally walked back into the room and then in one instant, bang, just like that, in one question—in the way she put one question, in the way she posed it, in the pose she took up as she put it—the whole thing fell into place.

Her corduroy coat was flung open. Her fist on her hip. She asked Julian "So who do *you* think was on the phone? I suppose you think it was Josh?"

Thereafter, it was Christabel who put the questions to Mozart. She began: *You've heard it all, Mozart, or very nearly all of it and you keep asking me to explain certain bits again only because you have a theory. It's now time I heard the theory.*

He answered: When we first looked at Julian's reaction to your trip with the Mimic we saw that your action had given him confidence to live. Now, I have to presume that we're looking at the same thing.

Julian is again trying to get away from death, and rightly or wrongly he considers Sally to be nearer life than you.

You mean younger?

No, come on, you're not old. That's not the point. You are old in only one thing. You are old in the knowledge of Julian's sickness. You've gone the whole way with it, and no matter how hard you try now, you cannot win the game he plays with you. That moment you remember so clearly, when he talked of fatal illness as a marginal example of the ageing process, even if it were undramatic at the time, is highly significant. When he said "fatal" illness to you and you went on arranging the flowers the game was up between you.

Perhaps it's much simpler than that, Mozart. Perhaps he never loved me, which would account for his reasonable reaction to the Mimic. But he is in love with Sally.

A-ha. I knew this one was going to come up. I cannot disprove it, but I can help you put it to one side and demonstrate to you that it is so unlikely as not to be worthy of our serious consideration.

You have brought in magic. In your fear and panic you have brought in hoodoo. Until now we've been having a rational talk about things. I don't care whether you call it philosophy, psychology, or what it really is, namely constructive gossip. Now you say "Ah" but maybe all our calculations are wrong because they may have drunk of the magic potion. It is exactly the same as saying "God's

on their side". Perhaps God was with our lot at Bannock-
burn, in which case he didn't half let us down later. If you
want to bring faith or magic in, there is no point in our
talking any further. You'd better pray or go and bury
your wedding ring under an oak-tree. It likely all happened because you walked under a ladder when you were
wearing green.

All right, all right. But there is such a thing as love.

Not agreed. There are at least fifty different things carelessly filed in our heads under the general section of love.
What we are talking of, here, or what you are afraid of, is
a case of obsessional love: the Albertine syndrome is what
the Americans would call it. The sort that finally makes
a man shoot himself over the lady's grave because his
energies are exclusively devoted to the pursuit of one
object—another person's soul. You are right to be afraid
of it. It does not reason. It is not something I have been
afflicted with myself, nor ever wish to be, but in jealousy
one gets an inkling of it. On the other hand I have seen it,
and I admit there are aspects of Julian's behaviour that
remind one of it.

Before we are infected, by love or measles, we are wide
open to infection. Yet we are obviously not always like that.
In the ordinary course of life we enjoy a certain degree of
immunity from our enemies, the viruses and bugs. When
we succumb, something in the balance is wrong.

We also know that the world would be an impossible
place to exist in, were we all to behave like Proust's nar-
rator when he was afflicted by the passionate attachment
to Albertine. It would seem to follow, then, that a certain
anti-social condition exists the moment before this kind of

insatiable attraction hangs a man up. If we want to save a friend therefore, and it is usually some husband, it is no good our saying "Be your age" or "Okay you've had a good run, now away home and make it up with Dorothy." His answer will always be the same. "It's impossible. You don't understand what love is." Which insults us, so we lose the friendship too. Actually he wants to lose the friendship, because that's yet another proof of his passion for the loved one, but we mustn't stray into all that.

The point I am making is that the only way to cure a man who is consumed by this kind of passion is to inspect the conditions that existed before he took the jump, then change them. People understand this instinctively by saying "We'll go away for a cruise and put the whole thing behind us." But that's usually a very transparent, false kind of change. There really does have to be a change.

Mozart, Mozart, stop. You are pursuing the most desperately depressing line. You are forgetting that the only change we can make to Julian's condition is to provide him with life and he is dying. I know he has only a very short time to live.

Were that the truth, I would still pursue it, and, if you wanted, you could walk away. No conclusion we reach can be very happy with regard to Julian's long-term chances. But this is not a medical council. What you do not see is that you have already instinctively done the only thing you could do to bring him back to you, which is presumably your desire.

I'm losing you.

It's very simple. In the first place you did not stop him

taking the Anglo-Scottish, First Class flight. Excellent. He expected you to do so, because he assumed that you would be frightened that the exertion would kill him. Second, you did a very nasty, female crafty thing. I witnessed you do it. That's where I came in. At the end of that awful cabaret in the pool you and Sally had a moment together out of Julian's earshot. In that short exchange you said "You had better know that he only has a few weeks to live." True or false?

True. And Miss Cohen replied "Not with me he hasn't."

Never mind her reply. The point is that up to that moment she never saw that he was that seriously ill. She behaved, therefore, in a normal way. In fact, it seems that we are witnessing one of those peculiar repetitions that happen in life. She has done for him exactly what you did when you went to bed with the Mimic. She has become more or less engaged to the Joshua Reynolds character, thereby proving to Julian that she sees him as a man, not a death's head. He probably does not perceive this repetition of himself. To see it clearly would be to undermine his only hope. His energies are therefore applied to knocking Reynolds.

You have now played a very dirty trick. You have given the girl the name of the game. She will never play it again therefore with such brilliant, careless accomplishment. Now she knows that he is dying she will have to play your games and she will not be so good at them as yourself. You have not exactly changed the conditions under which Julian contracted the obsession, but you have destroyed the escape route. You have fixed it so that the obsession itself is no different from at home.

Your Julian is no fool. The more you stare the more you see the truth in his remark that fatal disease is not separate, but just a marginal example of our usual carry-on. When middle-aged men push off with a young girl who then has a baby, their new house again becomes the kind of home they so wanted to leave in the first place. You've packed that one into twenty-four hours. Wherever they are now, this couple, I can tell you the general direction of their travels, any moment now. If we sit here for a day or two, they will either come through that door or you will get a phone call from a number near Oxford.

Which explains my previous personal note [he concluded with a sad grin] that it will be Mozart here who is the loser.

Chapter Nine

Aɴᴅ it is hard to have to report that Mozart, though Glaswegian, was not infallible. Events didn't come about precisely according to his oracular predictions. He had underestimated the other lady.

Sally and Julian were still in the Captain's Cabin.

"Well?" she asked.

"I'm sorry, love," Julian said. He was up, dressed, sitting in the armchair. On his behalf she had borrowed a pair of matching socks and a yellow shirt to go with his chinaman's face.

Sally looked quite angry. "There," she said. "You haven't listened to a word I said."

"Actually I was writing a couple of notes."

But he was caught out. She grabbed his note book and pointed at one of his hieroglyphics. "What's that?"

"It's an epsilon representing the elasticity of demand."

She said "Sorry I spoke." She was sitting on the rug at his knee. She went on sulkily "I was asking you when you made up your mind."

"About you?"

She banged her fists angrily on his knees. "Yes me. Sally. D'you remember me?"

He said "I'm out of pain."

She smiled at that. She put her chin on his knees and said "I told you. But don't talk about it. Answer my question, or I'll get bored. Me, me, me, me, tonight... When?"

"When I first set eyes on you."

"Oh Julian, no. I mean this time. When you came round to Half Moon Lane the other night... You went to the hotel, you had your Cutty Sark, you knew I was going with Josh, but when you came round had you made up your mind 'I'll take her away'?"

"No."

"I didn't think you had. You really just came to do what you'd done before, stir it all up, me especially."

"Yes."

"You know Josh is very big."

"I look very sick. He wouldn't hit me."

"Sid hit you."

"Well. Well, that wasn't very sore."

"Let me see your eye." She reached up and pushed his head to one side. She inspected closely. "You have got a bruise."

"Not as many as you have."

"Now—"

She began again, insistently:

"When, then? When did you make up your mind?"

"Well the answer is exactly the same as the first time." He replied slowly. He was still scribbling down some notes. "I told you. When I first set eyes on you."

"I think it was when Simon said ever so nicely how it

would be best if he rang your home. He thinks you're a dipso, he told me that. I think it was when you told them 'All right, ask Christabel to come', you must have made up your mind, really."

"No. I don't remember that."

"You were lying in the corner with all the records spilt about the place. After Sid had clonked you."

"I don't remember."

"Yes, you do."

"And you don't listen to me."

"How?" she asked. "You just said 'When I first set eyes on you' and that doesn't make sense. You mean when I first came back in? In the bedroom?"

"You were foul."

"So you don't mean that?"

"And you were even fouler when we went through and watched that television."

She laughed. She said "Yes. I wasn't very welcoming."

"You were foul."

She stood up and kissed him on the lips. She said "Couldn't we have more champagne?"

"There's some left in the bottle."

She was surprised. "You have changed."

She poured more in the glasses, then came back to sit by his feet.

He said "In the morning."

"When?"

"After Christabel arrived. You threw all those shelves about the place."

"You didn't love me for that?"

"Listen, child. Listen."

"All right. Go on. I want to know."

"Christabel went into your bedroom—then when she emerged, the phone rang for you."

"That was Shelley. It wasn't Josh. I told you that when I come back in the parlour. Remember, I asked you 'And who do you think that was on the phone?' And you just stared at me. Then you sat down, had some of your bloody medicine. But I said then. Or I said to Jacky how it was Shelley. The nerve of it, she was ringing to ask me 'Is it true you talked to Tom at his office yesterday?' . . . As it happens it was true. He can get tickets for 'Palladium and Josh wanted to go, so I rung him about that. Shelley goes on and on saying 'You keep your hands off my Tom. I had enough of this. It's Sally this and Sally that.' And I haven't even seen Tom since Easter. I don't know what's wrong with her. Mum says she can't seem to have a baby and Tom is a bastard, we all know that, but I don't see how she has to take it out on me. Specially down the phone at eight o'clock in the morning when I'm trying to catch a plane to Glasgow and I just been beaten to pulp."

"Oh darling, not pulp."

"Oh darling, yes pulp. And that's the last time for that, that's part of the deal. Promise."

"No."

"Julian, I'm not joking. If you raise a hand on me, I'm going."

He raised his hand.

She said "Anyway, you still haven't explained."

"Yes I have. And you missed it. When you came downstairs from the phone you were wearing the corduroy coat."

"That one—" she nodded towards it, where it hung behind the pine door. "Yes."

"It makes you look taller. You put one foot out in front of you in a way you never would have done last year. And I saw what you are, not what you were, for the first time. And I thought 'I wanted that other, first girl more than anything else in the world, at that time... But that was nothing, when I compare it with my love for this one.'"

"You mean you saw me different."

"Yes."

"Maybe Josh made me different."

He said "We're going to have to have rules about the names Christabel and Josh. But maybe the presence of Josh changed you. If it hadn't been him it would have been someone else."

"You can't blame me for that, now, can you?"

"I'm out of pain."

"Shsh." She kissed him, at once.

Of course we know more about ourselves than we used to do. But that only makes things worse, because we still do not know enough. In our insistent search to discover more about ourselves (Give us this day our daily analysis) we become more baffled than before. We are like archaeologists who dig to discover an ancient city and find traces and fragments of seven separate inconsistent cultures. The only homogeneity is geographical. The cities were built on one hill. The men are within one frame.

Privileged men are obliged to play a single predominant rôle more or less worthily. They are born kings or converted to a Faith. The rest of us have to live with all our personae. We juggle as father-figures, thinkers, husbands, poets, lovers and men of action. The less interesting have a shorter list of parts to choose from. Men like Julian— intelligent and passionate men—have the wider repertoire and need the greater energy and discipline to live with all their souls. But the sickness itself seemed to have corrupted Julian's will to play any rôle purely. He found himself abandoned to inconsistency and clinging, without sense of order, to the part closest to hand; often a violent part.

Aware of the dangers, of the merging of the rôles, the mixture of dream and reality, the loss of responsibility and the appetite for things red and black he moved like an actor in a play, a little unfamiliar with an inconsistent, murderous rôle. But he knew he couldn't go back. Sally had led him this far.

When he was fully dressed, and still out of pain, she and he walked out of the hotel, across the road, out on the stony shore of Loch Earn. The water was very still as a storm approached from the west. There was hardly a movement by their feet. But dark clouds over the jagged rims of the mountains were lit now and then by flashes of lightning; flashes that lingered at the back of their eyes. For a while they threw flat pebbles on to the water to make them skiff. Julian was very fond of the game.

Then half ironically, but compelled probably by the intense expression on Sally's face, he found himself proposing to her. He added, of course, "When we can fix up the Christabel complication and all that"... But in essence it was a direct proposal. "Will you marry me?" He seemed to mean "for eternity", seemed to be saying "I want you, not Christabel, in my grave"—then to shrug it off with a smile.

She took him completely seriously. She paused for a second as if she had been waiting all her life for him to ask her that much. She did not read his question as an invitation to the grave, but to life. A vivid flash of lightning made her jump and cry with fright. Then she stumbled forward and flung her arms round his neck saying "Yes" thirty or forty times.

The truth was that Sally, who would not have gone near the stage or cinema, who posed, blushed and ducked out at the thought of a camera, was probably one of the best actresses alive. She played the piece. She'd played the piece with Josh and played it with complete sincerity. Her present act with Julian didn't strike her as betrayal; didn't worry her at all. The programme had changed back. That was all. The Rep had put on Julian again. And now, in this part she was beginning to show real style. She had the absolute knowledge of his death; the absolute knowledge, in other words that this was the stage; that the play had a limited season. But she also had absolute faith. For her, on this stage there was no limitation of reality.

Mozart, therefore, could not have been further wrong in his assessment of her likely performance: it went beyond a game of bluff. No doctors, not Christabel, no colleagues, no trained sisters had anything approaching Sally's integrity in this play.

It was a grotesque double harness. She had not failed to hear what Christabel said as they parted. She knew in that split second that Julian was not even weeks away from the end. And yet his death now would come as an appalling, unexpected shock: a whole divine betrayal.

The games we play. Holding her by that lochside, as she trembled at the joy of the marriage that lay before them, Julian thought "We never, never succeed in removing all the veils. How clever I thought myself, in making for Half Moon Lane, how bright I was to know that the sight of her happiness in Reynolds's world would sting me back to some kind of night that did not start with a hot-water bottle and end in a chamber pot. Yet, something much more profound has happened. It is indeed the only kind of miracle in which I could believe. It is as if she saw me dying, in my seat in the stalls, this Rachel, this common Bernhardt, this Marie Bell, and she stepped off the stage. There was a moment of pandemonium, then she took me by the hand and led me into the play. Within that drama, her drama, I am not a dying man. She is saying with her eyes and her lips and her thundering heart 'While you play up here you exist up here, you have therefore immortality. The characters in the play do not die.' "

With genius, she had brought a lifetime to him in a matter of hours when he had in truth merely planned to use her sexiness and engagement to Reynolds as an antidote to pain.

Oh, there are still great, extraordinary moments in life. The game had style. The lightning flashed beyond Vorlich and to the west. And the first rush of wind disturbed the black water. It rustled the trees until they sounded like a distant audience of all the ancients, applauding a play.

Only twenty-four hours later, Sally was to tell Mozart about the subsequent events. She never described their host Matthew without bursting with laughter. Something about his size, or his accent or his bogus Scotch aggression quite bowled her over. For instance when they returned to the hotel that night she asked Matthew why he was dressed in a boiler suit.

He only had to reply "It's no' a boiler suit, it's dungarees" for Sally to double up in pain, with laughter.

So Sally told Mozart, when later they met: "Matthew was ever so nice . . . Mind, when I first saw him on that awful aeroplane I was crying because I thought we were going to be late. I mean, there may have been other reasons, but that was what it seemed like to me. I've always been scared of being late, especially at swimming comps.

"On the plane, I thought Matthew was horrible. Quite frankly, I thought 'What a typical big oaf of a Scot. The only thing he hasn't got is the red face.' And so bloody aggressive. Scotland this and Scotland that, but I see now he wasn't really like that at all. He had nice kind green-brown eyes. And his face was lovely. It looked like a big baker's or miller's and I suddenly saw he was sort of Dad. He was joking with us, the children, all the time. When Julian was bad up there, the first few hours, he was wonderful, Matthew, just lovely to me.

"Anyway, when we went inside, after the lightning and the lake, the wedding wasn't a bit as we'd imagined it from upstairs. It looked like a Sunday licence place, a lot of people soaking in drink to get their money's worth, others all dressed up looking glassy and hot, eating cookies and sausage rolls. Matthew was serving behind the bar and he'd put his dungarees on to bring up another barrel of this special beer he's got. Some kind of lager which Julian drank and liked. Well, Julian caught my eye where we're sitting on the stools and I had to lean right forward and take his hand because I thought I'd fall on the floor laughing. They were all so respectable and terrible and

old, and not what we'd thought, that I got absolutely un-
controllable giggles. Matthew spotted it and he begins to
giggle too. 'Oh Christ,' he says. 'Look at the cream of
Scotland, at Gerry Logan's nuptials.' Then he shouted
right out at them, 'What a lot of bloody deadbeats you
all are.'

"Well, Julian's ever so much better. We three start
knocking drinks back and we tell Matthew how we're
going to get married and Julian's eyes are never off me, I
can feel them, and he's saying when I look, 'I'm out of
pain. There's no pain.' And I was saying 'Speak for yourself' because the bar stool caught me on a certain bruise I
had on my behind. He'd inflicted that and he kept kissing
my ears now asking forgiveness and Matthew was the
beard, you know, how couples get a beard—one kind of
big friend in the know.

"Next thing we've slipped out of this lounge place and
get in the shooting-brake. We drive all the way to Glasgow, and it's still thunder and lightning. I'm hanging on
tight to Julian, all three of us in front, me in the middle,
Matthew also playing silly gear games with my knees.
Flashes of lightning lit the three of us up, like day.
Neither Julian nor I can understand half Matthew says
and his stories are terrible, all Scottish and pauky and
out of the ark. We told him that, too, and he gets the
giggles, too. On the way there we must have swallowed a
bottle of Scotch.

"Now, I don't know exactly how we come in, the
Trossachs or something. We join like at the bottom of
Loch Lomond and there's no rain yet over here . . . If you
know the road, you come round and up and then quite
suddenly you see all the lights of Glasgow below stretching

right as far as the docks and the river and that. So Matthew starts singing terrible Glasgow songs, then it was me who sees a glow and I said 'That's a house on fire.' For a while they thought it was maybe some kind of steelworks or refinery or something because there's a lot of those flaming chimneys you get.

"But it isn't. It's in the residential part. Well, of course, we can't resist that. Old Matthew drives right there, or as near as we can get and there are hundreds and hundreds of people in the streets. They're all lit up by this fantastic glow. And there's ever so many police, police vans, even mounted police, like for riots, and I'm far enough gone to say 'Yippee, let's have a go.'

"Matthew has no idea what it's about, but trust Julian. He asks Matthew 'Would this be Maryhill?'

"Answer, yes. 'Aye, aye.'

" 'I think we may find it has to do with the students at the Allan Ramsay School of Drawing.'

"He's amazing. How the hell he knows these things, and remembers them, beats me. He said he'd read of it in *The Times*. But Matthew and I hate police. We've got that in common. He hates them for all sorts of reasons to do with their actions in some Nationalist demonstrations, but I just hate them. Jacky once said she'd fallen in love with a policeman and I told her 'Don't think I'm prejudiced but you're out, the minute you bring a copper in here.' They beat people up, they do. And they take advantage.

"Anyhow, because Matthew thinks the police are bastards too, which is fine, he and I start down this kind of main road, then reach the dense crowd. It was ever so exciting. What's happening is that the school place which is on the corner of a big wide kind of terrace, with trees in the middle, almost like a square—it's burning like hell. All the fire-engines and police is trying to get at it but the students, ever so craftily, have built a bloody great barricade and they're not letting fire-engines nor nobody through. They want the bloody place to burn. They're throwing stones, bricks, anything to hand and the police is using the fire-hoses. Every now and then they grab some poor boy by the hair and belt the life out of him and then bung him in the black van. Behind them there's rafters crashing down, sparks flying, people booing, cheering, yelling and screaming, ambulances ringing bells. I never seen anything like it in my life. 'Isn't it *great*,' I kept saying, squeezing Julian's hand and he was looking intense like he gets, taking it all in, also very impressed by what he saw. I said 'Why didn't someone say. I never knew Glasgow was like this.' Next thing, I said, 'We won't get through this way.'

" 'What do you mean, through?'

" 'Through to our side,' I told him.

" 'You mean with the students hurling bricks and stuff?' he asked.

" 'Yes I do.'

"He nodded. For a moment he didn't seem too sure. He says to me 'There's a bead of sweat on your upper lip,' and he kissed me.

" 'Come on 'en,' I said, 'aren't you coming?'

"He was still looking at my mouth an' he said 'Yes'."

Julian did not have the same hatred of the police that possessed Sally and Matthew. Nor did he really have too much sympathy with students who accepted grants and went on strike. But his rational persona seemed to be already dead. Passion has spoilt more than one head. His motivation was therefore illogical, even foolish. At most there was an irreversible chain of events which matched the fury of the crab. Life was not connected by causal action any more but joined contiguously by a series of risingly exciting and destructive scenes. They could only end in hell. In other words, if asked why he went to Half Moon Lane in the first place, Julian could have answered "For an alternative in pain: for a life made vivid by jealousy." Asked why he had assaulted Sally to whom he had always previously been almost absurdly gentle he could have answered "Because she said that she had a nice holiday in France and I saw the sunburn line on her breast just as she told me that Josh Reynolds had taught her to fly." Asked why he had been so extraordinarily cruel to Christabel, treating her as if she were a servant on the plane, and an enemy at the pool, he could have answered "Because I'd beaten up Sally and she was crying and I was worried about her." Behaviour like matter is constantly subject to irreversible change. Asked why he had proposed to Sally, he could have replied "Because there was thunder and lightning and I was out of pain." Asked why he followed the other two round to the students' side of the barricade he could not honestly have replied "Because I'm a reformist" or "Because I've come to the conclusion that political change which is necessary to our eventual survival and happiness only seems to come about, these days, through social agitation." That thought had once occurred to the rational man inside him, but had been discounted by the same reasonable fellow who knew that violence breeds violence. Asked why he went to the far side of the barricade, and Julian was not so far gone as to ask himself just that, he could only reply with honesty "I tasted the salt on her upper lip."

Matthew led them past the nervous householders in Ramsay Gardens until the heat of the fire struck them on their faces. Many people shouted warnings but Julian took Sally's hand and pressed on until at last they reached the less impressive back or rearguard barricade. It was mainly constructed of overturned motor cars. Climbing between two of these, Julian shouted "Oxford" and signalled that Matthew was also a friend.

As they climbed over, the fire crackled and some sparks flew down quite close to them. Sally also was trembling with fear. Her eyes were black and burning bright.

"In'it *beautiful*?" she said.

Julian was not talking about the barricades, nor the dilemma of the students but at Sally's bright eyes when he heard himself reply "Life!"

Chapter Ten

PHYSICALLY, Mozart was lying on his back. Mentally he was at that borderline when it only needed a woman to say "You're snoring" for him to reply, quite truthfully, "I know."

But next door, in the bedroom, Christabel had other noises to keep her awake. The cats were wailing at wandering nocturnal gangs: at Handy Barr and Co. Four or five fire-engines suddenly crashed by, shaking the whole house. They were on their way to Ramsay Gardens, but she wasn't to know that. For her they were just another enemy of rest. She moved through to the front room.

She asked "D'you mind if I come in?"

Mozart was on the surgical bed. He was wrapped in some quilted sleeping-bag left over from the stocks of camping kit. He shone a torch on the lamp by the fireplace and she stumbled through the flotsam towards it, to click on its dicky switch.

He said "Sure, you come in. So long as you don't jump on me. I'm a moral boy."

"Oh Mozart, you can stop that, right away," she replied wearily.

He said cheerfully "I'm the loser. That's the terrible truth."

"Well what do you expect, if you keep taking girls back to the same cinema?"

Mozart sat up and searched for his glasses. He said "Oh no, it was a different cinema. A different show. Just that same bloody hunk of meat playing gymnastic love scenes here, there and everywhere. When he wore tights, they stuffed oranges and bananas and things down there I'm sure, just to make me sweat."

"Jealousy is not the best topic, Mozart. Tell me where the instant coffee is, and we'll talk about referees. You did leave that note at the Central Hotel?"

"Yes. For the fourth time: I did."

"I'm sorry."

"Och, he'll be there by morning."

Christabel sometimes picked her own paragraphs. She said "I don't quite understand whether you work at that pool every day, or were you just judging there?"

He eased out of bed. At night he wore no shirt but long underwear; combinations cut off at the waist, which reached down to the calves of his legs. He had an excellent figure.

"Mozart, you are an original," she said, taking in the costume. "You never fail to impress me."

"Pass me the oranges, hen," he said, through a big jersey which he was pulling over his head, "and I'll make you dizzy."

But she was beginning to lose heart. She hardly had the energy to smile. She looked older, an hour before dawn.

She said "Mozart, I can't spend the rest of my life sitting about listening to you."

"No. Not the rest of it." He drew back the curtains. He sat by the window. Then, still trying to cheer her he started to play his clarinet. To play jazz and other things: tunes, sweet and profound unglorious tunes. Dawn broke.

"God help us," he said, "the rain's stopping and it's going to be another sunny day. That's not right in Glasgow. Hark."

He pushed up the window and cupped a hand round his ear.

He said "Hark, I hear the starlings. We can with honour have a gin. It must be nearly five o'clock."

She took some persuading. She resolutely refused to have a raw egg in it. It wasn't the gin but the offer of the gin that diverted her just when cold reality was creeping in. It unlocked her. Solemnly, she began to talk.

She said "I suppose this is the first time I've gone two whole nights without a wink of sleep. Really I'm not so tired. Not fuzzy at all. I suppose it's like this in a battle. Oddly, I have the feeling of being more completely wide awake and sober than ever before."

"Also like battle."

"You haven't been in battle?"

"They sent me pheasant shooting in Korea when I was a very young boy. You do have the sensation of sobriety. That also was where I developed a lasting taste for sheer neat lovely gin." He swallowed a gulp at the thought.

She said "Quite apart from the battles, one has the feeling that a long, wakeful stretch like this is something which must occur at least once in someone's life. It is in its stillness that I realize for the first time what a serious business it all is. I don't think that's purely meeting you, though you have helped. When Julian was ill I was restless. When I discovered what was wrong with him, I had what are called sleepless nights, yet they were not wakeful ones like this.

"While you've been playing, I have tried to analyse why I feel this wakeful serious way, right now. To say it is a crisis is to understate it. But I know that Julian's death is a worse thing, or the death of one of my sons would be a worse thing. These deaths would not engender this same strange, wakeful mood. When I broke up my first marriage I had nightmares, drugs and Julian. But it seems that a marriage is consummated only in happiness. The more you talk the more you depress me because I feel that I have indeed made Julian also live wrongly; but however wrongly we or I have lived, we have together passed some years of gaiety and happiness. I hope they were not too much at other people's expense. They were not felt to be that at the time. It is these years of happiness, simply years lived with summer following on spring, with bills and plumbers and trips to London that seem to break my heart now. And if I speak so carefully like the Queen, let me sound like that, this once. In my country, in my world, I am on the brink of horrifying defeat.

"My plan on that aeroplane was to act with generosity. I know what the drugs alone have done to Julian. I know that he has in pain become somebody different from my Julian. I know he is dying. He either does or doesn't, but at least he pretends to himself and to others that he is not. So I said to myself, 'Don't be a dog in the manger. If he has this obsession for that peculiar common pretty little bit of a girl, then let it run for what it is worth. It is better than his sitting in bed wrapped up in himself till the end.'

"We sometimes act as if our parents and teachers were alive within us. Which is to say that we act with a dignity but not in truth, and the strain in the long, wakeful hours becomes too much. It is not, alas, that we are weakening. It is that we are seeing things as they are."

Mozart sat very still throughout this extraordinary manifesto. She spoke almost as if she were dictating her will. She paused between each sentence. It was as if, throughout the long, wakeful hours, she had been composing this testament. Her voice was quite flat. Almost expressionless.

"If I were to describe my heart, and I do not mean the physical organ under my left breast, I would have none of those difficulties which beset philosophers when they argue about the ghost in the machine. My heart, I see now, is the design of my life, is the sense I have made of experiences invited and experiences thrust upon me. I see now that I have made much more sense of life than I recognized before. I am one of those women who had a divorce and who cannot understand a couple divorcing. The first marriage was not consummated in happiness; the days are not therefore marked on my heart. Every day of my second marriage is marked there. I did not feel them leave their stamp. But they did, and they made their own point of living. Their existence made my purpose. Those days past are no bigger or smaller digits than the days my sons still have in front of them. My life is my heart. My heart is my marriage. My marriage is my Julian. Had he died there would have been no confusion, only sorrow. But this, coming now, has been too much. There is no organization left. The fact of my being is waste. That's all."

*

Mozart did not dare move; did not play more music; did not dare raise his glass to his lips lest that motion would release him; would let out the awful shout within him. She was by the window now. She turned back her golden head. Her eyes were for once not shaded by her hair. They were translucent and marine. It was as if she were sitting on an English shore, watching all the little boats drift out, unmanned, to sea.

Mozart felt amazed, almost afraid. There was no mess, no darkness, no blood: just clear light. There was no foreground, no stage-dressing except the sky behind her; there was only woman's face. She was quite immobile. On her forehead there was a diagonal line running above her brow which he had not observed before.

"The couple," he said at last, and he actually looked at his feet and raised his heels once or twice, as if he were determined to press and keep himself firmly on the ground. "I've always suspected that the trouble is the couple. Your life should not have had that design. That should not be the mosaic of your heart. At the bottom there is the same flaw in every revolution in the West. People say 'The women'. It is the couple. Marriage itself is the fatal insoluble hitch. We've locked ourselves in duologues, in boxes. Maybe that's the sin."

He got no further. There was a creaking downstairs. A vague "coo-wee" noise. Then some footsteps on the narrow wooden stairs.

Julian walked in.

Christabel didn't move.

He didn't look too drugged but he was evidently in some pain. He tried to light one of his long cigars, very shakily. He said to Mozart "It's a long time since I've seen somebody in combinations. I'm feeling slightly giddy. Do you mind if I sit down?"

Mozart stood back, and very slowly and carefully Julian picked his way to the three legged armchair.

She didn't move.

His cigar had failed to light. He searched for his lighter in his pocket, again. As he did so he removed a box of pills and the bottle of jungle-juice which was still half-full. Full enough to kill three or four of Handy Barr's mighty young men. He laid his palm on the bottle as if it reassured him.

He said, at last, "It didn't work. If that's of any interest to you." He smoked and for a second closed his eyes. He leant back his head.

She didn't move.

He said "I got your note at the Central Hotel."

Mozart asked "Is Sally Cohen with you?"

"We'll have to talk about that," Julian quietly replied. But he did not take his eyes off his wife, now. He watched her, unblinkingly, where she sat, her face silhouetted against the sky and countless chimney pots.

Their attitudes were similar and strange. They seemed to find it very difficult to talk, yet neither wished to be un-civil. The silence embarrassed Mozart. He folded up his sleeping bag, then decided to go, but he was too nosy to move farther than the bedroom, which was out of sight but not out of earshot. While he was there the couple did not exchange a single word.

Mozart put on his track suit and plimsolls. In the mornings he used to trot down to Gallowgate and buy his news-paper there. He would sometimes have a cup of tea before trotting all the way back again. He reappeared in the front room to say that was his plan.

Christabel said "All right."

Julian tried to get to his feet. He smiled and said "I don't really see why we should commandeer your house. Perhaps I could ring for another taxi. We could go back somewhere."

"Is Miss Cohen at the Central Hotel?" Christabel asked.

"Not as far as I know. She might go there, I suppose."

"Why should she?"

"Well, she knows you were going to be there. But I . . . I don't think she'll go there."

"Where is she now?" Mozart asked.

"I'm not very sure."

"Were you in Glasgow last night?" Christabel joined in.

Julian shook his head and pushed his hair away from his forehead. He said "I don't think this line of questioning will lead us very far."

Again he closed his eyes and leant back and waited and tried to smoke. He was beginning to feel sick. Mozart left the room saying he would be away for a quarter of an hour.

Christabel went into the bedroom. She changed and brushed her hair. Julian seemed to find it easier to talk with her when he didn't see her.

He said "If I don't get back to Oxford will you speak to my colleague John Hodson. He's junior proctor this year. Tell him to organize dancing in the streets, drinking in the saloons and necking in the parlours."

"Oh yes?"

"The unpalatable truth about violent demonstration is that it has its own romance. Ninety per cent of the young men involved are only here because the girls want to be seen with the young men who go there. It's rather like uniforms in 1940."

"Do I take it that Miss Cohen also likes that kind of man?"

He didn't answer. Soon, she drifted into the front room. His eyes were closed. He'd fallen asleep for a moment. But he woke up again as she crossed back to her place at the window. She could see he was in pain.

He said "I had what's called an eventful night. Somebody got killed."

"Not her?"

"No. Our friend from Anglo-Scottish, First Class. Matthew."

"How?"

"Here in Glasgow," Julian said. "First, we were up at a place called Loch Earn."

"For the wedding of Gerry Logan?"

"Yes."

After a while he said, "Your friend here appears to be something of an athlete."

"He's a referee."

"How apt."

It was the only time Christabel smiled. She hadn't the energy to chuckle. She said "I suppose it is, rather." He reached for her hand but she kept it away from him.

It was as if they knew they had a scene to play and both were too intelligent to dodge it. Yet neither had the taste or energy for it.

Out of the blue she asked "Did you have any difficulty finding this place?"

He shook his head. With the weariest smile he added "I've always been rather good at tracking you."

If you live together long enough, you miss out half the links. She knew exactly what he was talking about. He was referring to her afternoon with the Mimic in the airport hotel, a year and an age before.

She said "I can see how you came to try an airport hotel. That's geographical. If I were to leave at lunch time it was obvious that I wasn't going as far as London. But there are three or four of them."

"I tried three or four of them."

"How did you know the name?"

"Because you told me you'd met an admirer of mine at St James's, that lunch you went to. Barrington Whatever. I wouldn't have remembered the name unless you'd said he'd gone on about me being bright. You'd be surprised how often I've told Miss Cohen of your virtues and your charms. We usually can't help being nice about people we're betraying."

He seemed about to say more, then he stopped and sighed. The cigar had gone out. He said of the jungle-juice "I'd better have a spoonful of this." It was funny that he did not swig it any more.

"Do you need it?"

"Frankly I think any man who finds himself in my situation would need it."

"You've only got this?"

"I've some pills."

She held out her hand. The rule was to keep the jungle-juice until the last.

He extracted his wallet from his pocket. He was in need of drug itself more than pain killer. The shakes they call "withdrawal symptoms" were very bad. They increased rapidly now. He hardly managed to get the wallet out of his pocket. When at last he did so it flew open and some of its contents fell on his lap and on the cushion of the chair. The pills were in a plain envelope.

As she helped him, she happened to pick up another object. It was a lock of hair. But it was not her hair. It was black.

She tucked it back in the wallet. He tried to explain something, went so far even as to suggest that it was one of the boys' and she didn't bother to say that it was a darker shade of black. She took the pills and the bottle which had fallen on the floor and went through to the bedroom where there was a tap and a sink.

With great difficulty he managed to get the wallet back into his pocket. He called to her and she did not come. He shouted. He began to shout in panic.

She was by his side with the pill ground and dissolved in a big spoon. He reached out for it and she said "Keep your hands down. Just open your mouth. Lean your head back on the chair." He obeyed. She put the spoon in his mouth and he swallowed and sighed.

At that point the shop door-bell rang down below.

Christabel returned to the next room and threw the spoon with a clatter into the sink. As Mozart appeared with the papers at the top of the stairs, Julian made some effort to control himself. He said faintly "Hello."

Mozart was reading the front page. He said "There's high jinks at the Allan Ramsay all right."

Julian said "I know."

As Christabel returned to the room he said "That must have been the fire-engines we heard."

Mozart, seeing her face, wondered what had passed between the two.

Julian said "Three or four fire-engines."

Christabel lay down on the surgical bed and closed her eyes. There were tears running down her cheeks.

Mozart said "And not just the riots, there's been a fire."

"I know."

"Two or three houses."

Julian sounded quite irritable, suddenly and illogically. He said "Yes I know. I saw it."

Mozart said "Christ we missed that. We never saw any—"

He was over by the window and he turned back to Christabel. She had rolled over and was facing the wall. She was shaking in a horrifying, convulsive manner. Mozart imagined she was sobbing.

Julian, seeing Mozart's expression, turned his head and looked vaguely towards his wife.

She exploded then, wailing and shouting something.

Mozart hesitated.

Julian closed his eyes and leant back. Mozart flung the paper aside and strode across to her. He rolled her over. Her eyes were open but blind. Some kind of spleen or plasm dragged from her mouth onto her clothes.

Mozart dialled Emergency and called an ambulance.

He dashed through to the pantry and found the empty bottle which was labelled quite literally "Jungle Juice" with an exclamation mark.

"How much was in this?" He shook Julian by the shoulder and pushed the bottle in his face.

"Too much."

"What is it?"

"They don't tell me."

"But what?"

"If they come quickly she has a chance." She was groaning again.

"Oh Christ save us," Mozart was saying, tearing at his hair.

Julian said "That little girl was at a hotel called the Kenilworth."

Mozart went back to the bed and held onto Christabel to prevent her rolling off it. He sat her up and banged her back. He was not so good in this crisis as he had been before. He was crying and shouting, trying to tell her to be sick.

Then he asked Julian "What was it she said? What did she shout?"

Julian replied, very faintly, "It sounded like 'Peek-a-boo'."

Chapter Eleven

SALLY took a taxi down to the Swimming Baths immediately Mozart called her and she arrived at the
Aytoun Bath, the competition pool which he supervised,
shortly after noon. Some school children were on their way
out of the place. She pranced past them in her most self-
conscious way. Indeed she was so embarrassed by their
stares that she failed to recognize the lobby in which she
had played one of the biggest scenes of her life.

She went through the swing doors with their handsome
polished bars and followed the sign down a wide shadowy
corridor with walls painted green. She stepped down into
the old Aytoun Bath which was laid out in a strange way.
Its entrance was at the side of the clock gallery where some
fifty spectators could sit. A dozen steps led down to the
bath itself. The changing rooms, "Men" and "Women",
were each side of the showers and the drying rooms which
had once been operated as a Turkish bath. The three main
tiers for spectators lay along the length of the bath at the
far side. The roof was constructed of ironwork and three
domes of glass. The pool was well appointed but, built
early in the century, fatally reminiscent of a public lava-
tory.

Two or three assistants were cleaning the sides of the pool under Mozart's cheerful and rude directions. He came round the end of the bath and shook hands with Sally quite formally. He led her into his own office which had a window overlooking the pool. It was situated at the bottom end, opposite the clock, and marked firmly, "Mr A. Anderson".

She asked outright, "Is she dead?"

"No."

Before she could put the next question, he said "She'll pull through now. Quite quickly. They say she's a strong girl."

"Oh that's good."

"She is also a very nice girl, a great girl. I hadn't met her until the cabaret here in this pool, but I have spent a good deal of time with her since then. I have a high respect for her. I thought I'd better make that clear."

"Is Julian coming down?"

"He is at the hospital."

"At her side?"

"I don't know if he's at her side."

"It'll take it out of him."

"Yes. Yes it will. It's my lunch hour. Would you like to go out and eat something?"

"That would be nice."

She gave nothing, absolutely nothing away. She looked very tidy; though round the neck not very clean. Her suit was pressed, her nails polished, her shoes bright green. They were brand new. She sometimes carried her bag carelessly like a schoolgirl, bending her elbow and letting her wrist fall back, taking the weight of the strap.

Mozart thought "Mozart, you called this one a little bitch and no wonder you called this one a little bitch."

She said "D'you drink?"

"I do."

She said "Maybe we could go to a pub."

"I'm surprised at a national competitor like you taking alcohol with—"

"Oh, that's all over. I'm never going to swim again. Not competitively I mean."

"You've no ambition?"

She said "I've taken a fancy to booze."

"Ah," Mozart said and thought to himself, "Mozart, be fair. This girl is of a lower class than Julian and Christabel; of a class, in fact, no different from your own and you are often criticized for your off-putting manner. Moreover there is a sexual factor here. She may seem even more of a bitch to you because her shape alone—never mind those black eyes—is a challenge. It is not possible to look at her without wishing her on the floor with her ankles round her neck and the Mozartian elbow up—Be fair, Mozart, be fair."

"What can you put in gin apart from tonic?" she was asking as she walked along. "I don't like that quinine. Besides, it's fattening."

"That doesn't need to worry you."

She turned. "Doesn't it?"

Point to Miss Cohen. The wee bitch. Mozart blushed and frowned and lowered his head. To think such thoughts at such a time. The nerve of that girl, to use all that . . . Watch your eyeballs, Mr M.

"Gin's a London drink really, in'it?"

"Not exclusively," Mozart said.

"So I notice."

He had chosen a hotel bar because he was in his track suit and he knew that they wouldn't like that. But there was no row. He had forgotten about his companion. There was no Glasgow door, confronted with that brown, pink, young, tough, sweet, naughty face, which would not open wide.

The trouble was in keeping the waiters away.

She put six cherries in her gin, then added ginger ale. It was an upstairs carpeted bar in a horrible hotel.

She said "Well, yes it was an eventful night. Is that what he said?" She smiled kindly at the thought of Julian. "He's a pig isn't he, wandering off like that without telling me? That's typical of him. Half of last year he spent saying 'Good-bye—good-bye' and I'd think 'Ahuh, see you Thursday'. But he shouldn't have done that here, I mean leaving me stranded in a big city like this. But he's a genius, in his way."

"What way's that?"

"I don't know. You don't like him, do you?"

"He was very polite this morning. But he does some odd things."

"I'll say. He's put me through the book."

"Is that why you went with him?"

"What, the sex? No. Though he's quite a surprise. No, I just fancied him. Then we went out. Then I loved him. Then I fell in love with him at Brighton. I was crazy about him. Then it was a bit strained after a while. I still loved him, but it wasn't all joy. Then we started playing all those good-bye games, taking each other to the precipice and hanging on like mad. Then he went. I heard nothing.

I went with someone else. Then he came back. I was getting really muddled. Then I could see the other one wanted to marry me and I began to love him. Fickle, I am. I fell in love with the other, too. Then Julian arrived in a heap and we had this awful time and came up here. Then Christabel said something to me."

"That he only had a few weeks to live."

"No."

"She told me she said that."

"Did she? Well, anyway it wasn't that which got me . . . That must have been out in the hall outside the pool?"

"It was."

"No, it was something else she said, just before I went down to change, I was standing at the bottom of the steps by the gallery there, just before you pulled me away, something she said when Julian had been raging at her. She said it to him really, but she knew I heard. She said 'Oh come on Julian'—you know that tone she's got—she said 'Let's face it, if you were in your right mind you'd see you'd soon get bored with that.' I don't like being called 'that'. Someone once called my mother 'a common little usherette'—not as a joke, mind—when my sister Shelley and I was just little, and we both heard. It reminded me, I suppose, her calling me 'that'."

"Christabel's not a snob."

"Yes she is."

"Look. It's pointless arguing."

"Yes it is." She agreed and took a sip to drink. Which made Mozart sweat.

He said "Look, she and I have spent hours together—"

"Maybe it's rubbed off. The snobbism, I mean."
Mozart blushed.

"You annoy me," Mozart said.
"Oh yes?"
"You annoy me, because you're like me—you're one of us."
"Ta." In a corner, she'd always caricature herself.
"Don't you think you've done any damage?" He was beginning to lose his temper. He said as much as she picked a cherry out of her glass, only he was so worked up that the word came out wrong, as "tember".
"Oooh. Tember, tember," she cried and fell about, giggling. He had to laugh too.
He said "Are you some kind of butterfly?"
"Yes."
"But doing these things and now picking out bloody cherries—"
"It's called living."
Mozart ordered more gin. She wanted Coca Cola with it this time.
"Oh no..." Mozart said.
No man ever handled the first rounds worse.
The waiter winked at Sally and went back to the bar.
"He's Spanish," she said, "isn't he? Maybe I'll spend my honeymoon in Spain."
"Who with?"
"Julian."
Mozart frowned. He was shocked, suddenly. He couldn't understand her blindness. He felt constrained to break bad news which must previously, in some incredible way, have been misunderstood.

"Sally dear, listen—"

Right along the line, she said "With Julian. When he's better."

She said "'Xpect you wonder why. I wonder why. I mean it's not really natural someone like Julian, someone like me. I see that. When I was with Josh I was thankful that way. Josh is athletic. He's not brilliant, but he's not dumb. He's certainly no more dumb than me. And he's a man. I mean a real man. If I went with someone else without telling him and he caught me that would be the end of it. And he likes friends. There's always half a dozen of us and it's—it's living . . . I'm out on the airfield, they go up and do this crazy sky-diving, falling for miles whizzing all around the big blue sky. I wouldn't do that, but he taught me to fly.

" 'He taught me to fly.' When I said that to Julian the other night when he come back, the night he arrived in Half Moon Lane . . . That's what set him off: 'He taught me to fly'. Up until that moment it had been all ever so polite and watching Sportsview in the parlour. This other boy's sitting with us most of the while and poor Julian's getting more and more glum. He had one of his pains I expect. But he never speaks about them. Like he hates me if I even have a headache. He just won't have it. I'm Sally, always healthy, always brown, always ready for more. He doesn't really see me as I am. But I see Julian, make no mistake. I see him better than Christabel or any of you, better than his mother I bet. That's where you all get it wrong. I don't care how old I am, I see him best.

"You should see him with his clothes off. No. Forget it. But that's funny too, isn't it? I mean Josh is a very good-looking young man. But he hasn't got Julian's eyes. He hasn't got Julian's look. Julian can frighten me. And sometimes, you wake up, you look over, you see Julian and really he's old as the hills for thirty-eight. But Christ, what a face. In the middle of the night, he's got the most beautiful face.

"I mean Josh takes ten times the risks Julian ever took every day. He's got guts and he's been in terrible trouble. Cool in crisis. All that. But he hasn't got the pain in his face. Even Jacky said that.

"'He taught me to fly.' When I said that to Julian the other night I knew it would hurt him. That's strange isn't it? Except we always played that game. I mean often he's said what Christabel was, what Christabel did. Not obviously, but slipped it in about her laughing, her not being absolutely faithful, but still being great. For months he needled me like that. But he never once got the knife in as far as I did in that one little blow: 'He taught me to fly'.

"'He taught me to fly.' Soon as I said it, I knew he was going to half kill me. Did I know. He just looked at me. Not blinking, his face very sharp and I thought 'Whoopee, that hit'. I went on and on about it. I was being foul to him anyway. I went on about flying, about the rudder and the trim and that. Really foul."

Mozart asked: *How foul? I mean foul, how?*

What? In Half Moon Lane? . . . Well . . . Where do we learn it? Even after this other boy had finished watching the game on Sportsview, when we were left alone, like, I was still being cold as anything, prancing about, tidying up, saying "Have you heard this disc, it's new, it's

French?" Meaning of course I got it on holiday. And he knew where I was on holiday and with whom and how it had been a lovely success. So I was flirting, teasing: that.

But it's worse than that. He was looking quite sick, old Julian. He'd taken his awful pills or whatever and same time I was saying "No. What, me? I'm engaged", flashing my new ring and all that, I was also saying "Well, if you're so mad about me, I suppose I might be so good as to let you make love to me, but don't think for one moment that anything hangs by that."

It's funny. It's hard to explain sometimes the complicated kind of way we act. I didn't think it up. It just happened that way. It was worse than "Who's sorry now?" If you see what I mean. I was saying—you don't mind me being frank, its usually Jacky I tell and she doesn't understand one word in ten—I was saying, "All right then, Julian. Tell you what. Taste it again. Go on. Taste it again. Stand me on my head. Tell me how you taught me. You did. I don't take that away from you. I don't have to. Taste it again Julian. I'll still walk the other way." Does that add up to foul?

That said, she held her forehead in her hand for a moment: even she seemed stunned by her streamlined cruelty. She muttered "Christ." Mozart was asking something about her intimate life with the two men.

She answered like this:

You mean, sex? Josh isn't an innocent... Hell... I mean I was confused at first because he couldn't be less like Julian. He doesn't give much away. Josh made me feel littler and safer. Things didn't always go right. Things don't always go right with Julian come to that, but it's not as if Josh doesn't care. He gets ever so worked up and worried if he doesn't think I've come through. He's no less sensitive. That's not true to say. Yet it's not altogether true to say how Julian's less of a man. They got different ideas of what a man should be, I expect.

Yes, I could love Josh again. I could fall in love with him again. I'd be better with him. My life would be much happier.

Why happier?

Why? Because Julian's Julian. Because Julian knows me like no one will ever know me, ever, ever. And I know him as he really is. Not Christabel nor anyone knows Julian like me. We started a game. This is my life, this game. I see that now. (Then, quite unaware of her contradiction, she added vaguely:) He doesn't know me at all, but he really looks for me.

And you look for him? Who do you find?

... You mean "Who is he?" You can't answer that. It's the same question as how do I come to fancy him enough to go off with him at this stage when I got someone like Josh on the hook? You can't answer it except as I've already said. Compulsion. Timing. I don't know.

Mozart tried to put the question more accurately as follows: *You have suggested that I don't like your Julian. I don't. I might have liked him before his illness—*

She interrupted: "What are you talking about, this illness?"

"Could I finish my piece?"

"Illness is nothing to do with it. Is it?"
"Could I?"
"All right."

*Meeting Julian now I don't like him but I feel I may have
missed something in him. When you say you love him you
add that you know him like nobody else knows him.
What is it that you know about him which Christabel and
others close to him do not know?*

Cripes. He's got a word for it. He's always got words
for things, spot on. And he knows things. It's really incredible what he knows but doesn't let on.

Last night, for instance, when we're coming away from
this Lochearnhead hotel and this wedding party which
was honestly a drag, I notice the dump's called "Craig
Dhu". I wouldn't remember it except I wrote it down in
my diary. Now you'd expect Matthew, he's the bloke that
owned it, he's the Scottish Nationalist that got burned to
death which was horrible really horrible, well you'd expect him to know what Craig Dhu means. But it's Julian
says "Good night at Black Rock".

I say "What are you talking about, then?"

We're all driving along in this shooting-brake, Matthew
in dungarees as a matter of fact. I say "What's it got to
do with black rock?"

"In Gaelic black rock is Craig Dhu," Julian says.

Matthew was very impressed too. He said "You've been
to Scotland before then," and Julian answers "No"...
Julian's like that. It's nice having someone who knows.
He never bluffs like everyone else. Either he knows or he
keeps his trap shut.

And one day in France, I must tell you this, one day in

France Josh and I were at one of these level crossings they got. He'd been diving and that, and we were going back to this hotel where we lived. It was hot. Quite hot. Well, a goods train goes by and on one of the wagons there's the letters E.P.V.—E.P.V. I'm sure of it. So I said to Josh "What d'you suppose E.P.V. is?" It was silly, really. He hadn't been looking at the train. He says,

"Why, that's extra sensory perception."

I said "No it's not."

He said "In America there have been a lot of studies on E.S.P., some of them at Berkeley," which is this college where he went.

Well, I know he's off net, so I just say "Not E.S.P.—E.P.V."

He quite ignored me. It's one of the only times he ever annoyed me. He went on about E.S.P., about cards and random numbers and Christ knows what. So I switched him off. He's happy. Maybe he majored in E.S.P., who cares. I was hot. It was hot.

And I thought as I sat there, and another bloody train went the other way, I thought I know exactly what Julian would have said. Julian would have said "I don't know".

And I thought. And I thought of Julian and I thought if I had a little boy, maybe two years old, or three, sitting on my lap in the car and he was watching this train go by at the crossing, I thought he wouldn't know where it was going to or where from and he'd watch it and like it, and I'd like him liking it, and tears came in my eyes. Because I do want a baby. I really do want a little boy.

As we drove on, I knew something. On my lap, it was Julian's little boy, taking it all in. Years later when I'm an old hag, I'll ask him, "What's E.P.V.?" and he'll be able to tell me. Because he's Julian's boy.

I swallowed all that at the time, of course I did. Except to shout again "E.P.V. *not* E.S.P." Then I kissed him better—Josh, I mean. He's like me, Josh. Ever so like me. He likes the same foods. Hates fish. Doesn't go for wines, nor do I, really. He's much more suited to me than Julian, I know.

Still Sally speaking:

Is "ambiguous" a word? I think that's it. Two things at once. Not one or t'other. Not either or neither. That's what I know about Julian, no one else does. I mean everybody can say "I know a side of him his wife doesn't". But I know more than that. I know what's wrong with Julian and there is something, I admit that. He's got this illness, off and on, whatever it is and he is brought right down, anyone can see that, but I know exactly why.

It isn't just Christabel and me, like blonde and brunette, though that's what it's come to, more or less. Julian's always asking me funny questions if we wake, say, in the middle of the night. He asks all sorts of things about Mum, or Jacky, she's my friend, or how ever I got into the bloody Air Ministry or why I think the Duke of Edinburgh's great . . . He made me find out if my grandfather really was Russian and as a matter of fact he was. He was the one as takes the name of Cohen so's he'd be nice and close to the top of the soup queue, Mum says, the point being that they worked alphabetical in displaced persons camps, or wherever—Julian loved that. "Why not Adler?" he said.

Anyway, as I was saying, he asks me questions and he

goes on about what he calls my myth. He really does love what I am. Does that make sense? He kind of looks at me, breaks me up into atoms or genes or whatever and blesses each one of them. Or kisses them, as a matter of fact, finding them in very strange places, which is nice. Julian was with me the first day I moved into Half Moon Lane and I was quite scared, I'd never lived alone before. It was a week or two before Jacky joined me there. He sniffed around that place. Julian loves Half Moon Lane. I can't get out quick enough. But not him. I'm not saying he doesn't love me. I'd be stupid if ever I said that. Julian really loves me. If I'm sure of anything on earth I'm sure of that. And I'm not so silly as to think that's nothing. I promise I'm not. When he did break from me, six months back, I wept and wept. I didn't believe he could or would. And I'm sure he cried. But he also loves everything about me, in a way; in a way; in not exactly an odd way; in a greedy kind of way.

I'm saying he had to find me. He was desperate to find me. And maybe I didn't disappoint him. For lots of other reasons I was looking for him, I expect. So we met. But he still couldn't do anything about it. He's such a simple ... I don't know. He's not capable of coming out and saying "Look, this whole scene is wrong for me". Not to Christabel or to me. It's the scene as much as me. That's what I know. But there's something else I know which they don't. He's fought my scene hammer and tongs. Christ, he's forced me to go to Josh, go half way to California. But I am his scene. I am. He's a good man, Julian, I know he is. He really loves not only me but people like me. I swear he does. And he really loves Christabel, I see that. But he hates her bloody scene. I promise he does. He's said as much when he's been drunk or drugged or whatever it is. Now put yourself in the middle of that, of course you don't know where you are, no matter how clever you're being in Downing Street or Oxford every day. And so what happens? He gets ulcers or whatever it is he's got. He goes down and down same as everyone goes down if they can't see the way through.

Why should I care? That's what amazes me. Why the hell should I care for this funny white bird, with Josh and everything lying the other way? I do care, terribly. Julian needs me. I didn't see it until that bloody swimming-pool. I've often thought "If it comes to it, I'll fight" but that wasn't serious, just imagining. Then suddenly she's in front of me, her face turned half away from me, saying really sincerely "You'll get bored with that" and. And. And, no. No: Julian's mine. Of course he is. No one, not you, not Christabel not even my bloody mother is going to take him away now.

Nor death. See?

Chapter Twelve

THEY sat talking long after they'd finished coffee and ham sandwiches: Sally and Mozart. Technically the licensed lounge should have been vacated at half-past two but Mozart was a special case in that he'd seduced the manageress on Hogmanay, 1965. He should have been back at work, but that didn't seem to worry him. He said the kids could drown themselves that afternoon in the Aytoun Baths.

Of course he was furious that he had missed the big drama at the Ramsay School. He kept taking Sally back to that, asking for more detail; asking, for instance, what happened once she, Julian and Matthew were what Mozart called "the right side" of the barricade. (Christabel would have tackled him on that.)

Not that Sally was too sure about the students' cause.

She said as much.

Said:

...I don't quite know what they were on about, these students, but it turns out they're not just the art school ones there. Anyhow this building is white hot now and right close. I'm scared, a bit, and there's big smuts and sparks come floating down. They found me a kind of helmet, and we take our sort of posts this side, not t'other where the main war is going on. Julian has to sit down and he couldn't have thrown a paper dart by this point, he's so weak, but 'is face is up against that burning light and I see the sight—just the excitement is doing things for him like it does for me. The students are all so young and set and scared but not showing it. As I say, I didn't know what exactly it was they wanted but I knew I was on the right side, and I knew Julian was too. And I have to admit, I think Josh would have been the other side of the barricade. The long way round the back of the gardens had taken a lot out of us and we sat getting our breaths back, when some group of police come into the square. We heard the householders cheering and clapping before we saw them.

They'd helmets on. And these bloody great batons in their hands. And they come in a line. I tell you, I never been so scared in my life. Yet you couldn't go back, see, not unless you wanted to go in the flames or get beaten up, the other side.

Julian was a bit crazy now. Maybe he thought the whole thing was part of a nightmare. Whatever, he threw the first brick. It didn't even reach them but that wasn't the point. You could see it in his face, he'd never thrown a brick at authority, never in his whole life. It made me smile, right there and then. Then we were all flinging things, hell for leather, at the bastards. They got right up to us, right between the cars, smashing the boxes and things down with their big feet and some of them got bonked too. Matthew threw two of them back so they got concussion, I think. Anyway. After a bit they fizzled out, really, and went back to regroup.

Then it happened. Just as we were getting warmed to it and laughing and saying how we'd won, this awful thing happened.

While we'd been fighting away, the house next door to the school had started to smoke from the windows like mad, then down below there was a belch of flame. All of a sudden we all saw this woman, screaming, up the top in what must have been the third or fourth floor if you count them kind of semi-basements. She's trapped in there for sure. Maybe she was deaf or something or had taken sleeping pills. She was miles up, but you could see the expression on her face. She must have been fifty-five or sixty, you know, and all puffy and not believing her eyes and scared, scared, scared.

Matthew simply walked straight into the fire. You know you hear of brave acts, you think "Oh he must have risked a lot going in as late as that." But I didn't understand what bravery was before. There was no question of going in. It was a fire, not a house, a fire. I mean it was minutes after the moment when a brave man might ask himself "Should I, shouldn't I?"

He never thought. Right through the bloody burning door and we all yelled. Some of the people came over from the other barrier. Some were shoutin' to let the firemen through. So was I.

You should have heard the cheer we gave when all of a sudden we seen him up there beside this woman and she throws her arms round his big neck. Matthew was Dad. I never knew you had Scotsmen like him, no wonder you're always in wars.

I don't really want to tell the rest. Julian and I stood there cheering and squeezing each other's hands and cheering and weeping. Maybe it all should have stopped just there, with big Matthew at the window lifting up the woman, all the students round about and Julian and I, tears streaming down our faces, looking up into the fire.

But it didn't end there. Evidently Matthew couldn't find a way downstairs again. They vanished, then appeared back at the window.

There was terrible confusion at the other barricade. The firemen weren't let through even then, which is the students', not the police's fault, even I see that... Whoever...

Matthew left the woman by the window for a moment. She looked down, looked back into the house. Maybe she fainted. If she jumped, she must have seen something white below and made a mistake. Because there was no sheet. No nothing. Except the iron railings round the basement and they had spikes.

Mind, she was stone dead. And some of the students, they lifted her off and there was blood and just about the same moment the firemen came through the other side and the police took their chance. They come pouring in behind. Suddenly, there's water and shouting and horses rearing about the place and no sign of Matthew, none at all. Then a big whoosh, like an explosion almost. The roof of this house goes up and Julian and I are on the ground in each other's arms being rolled over and over by the force of a hose. Someone drags us farther aside and we just hang on to each other, hang on, hang on.

When I open my eyes we're with two of the boys who was hurling bricks beside us and they get Julian to his

feet somehow and we start running and pushing and trying to get away from the horses. It was the horses scared
me. At last we got a bit of air. Julian h̄ad to be carried
by two of them.

We went into a house with an open door, some kind of
ambulance men were there. We were filthy. My coat's
thrown away, my tights and shoes ruined. Julian's panting, and panting. They give him something but he's not
unconscious and he's still got his hand in mine and he's
saying "No pain." I'm kissing him all over his face.

Julian lay in her arms amazed at the violence of his own
behaviour. She smelt of cinders from the fire. This building where they were now sheltering was called the Kenilworth Hotel. The light seemed very bright and the room
was filled with people, some of them bruised and some of
them burnt. All of them were very, very young. He and
Sally had found a corner. They were lying on a narrow
iron bed and he kept coming round, then slipping away.
He supposed it was sleep, but feared it to be the other
thing. He could feel her arm round his neck and she kept
kissing his eyes, then she slipped down and buried her
face somewhere in his neck and chest. He had no energy
to say the things to her which he now felt. He believed
the experience of the last hours to have been more brilliant
than any in his life. He dared not analyse why. They'd
found their scene in violence and together they were
afraid. It was right that he should die here, in her arms.
There was no pain at all.

The Kenilworth Hotel was normally a students' digs
but was the headquarters of the rebels at the Allan Ramsay. The ambulances had been organized, the medical

supplies had all been prepared in advance. There was even some cocoa.

But there was no rejoicing. All the kids were white-faced and exhausted. Some sat shaking, from excitement and shock. There were practically no girls, except the ones with the cocoa, and even the dressings and bandages were applied by men. All the rooms were open. All were full. The house was crowded out. Even the staircase was covered with boys half asleep.

Who the hell told the police to go to the Kenilworth, nobody ever knew. That's the sort of mistake that gets lost in the records. It was not difficult for the authorities to find out the significance of the Kenilworth, and the names of the ringleaders, but they could have picked these boys up any time. The motive must have been vengeance. The police had suffered as many casualties if not more than the students and one constable had been seriously wounded. His immediate superior evidently decided that insufficient numbers of the rioters had been apprehended.

A large squad went down to the Kenilworth, and moved into the house almost before the incumbents realized what had happened. One boy had the presence of mind to remove the mains fuse in the cellar. Others poured from windows, rushed out the back door: Chaplinesque.

Julian felt Sally's strong, sweet arms and legs clasping round him as she screamed and screamed not to be taken away. He felt the baton on his shins and his shoulder. She was yelling and fighting like a cat. The police were swearing and calling her names. Julian clutched one by the throat. Then he heard rather than felt the crash of a baton on his head, at the back. He tore the policeman's epaulette as he fell.

The epaulette was still in his hand when he came round. He was on the floor. There were only four or five of them left in the house. The ambulance men and himself. The cocoa girls.

There were still no lights and nobody had a candle or a torch. The ambulance men lit matches as they helped him out of the building to the ambulance itself. The fresh air brought him round again. He still felt very little pain except from the bump at the back of his head. The police vans had moved off. He was too weak to protest as he was carried into the ambulance and taken away. But in the ambulance he felt the epaulette in his fingers, still. The clip was sharp. The number was a strangely easy one to remember. It was 101R.

There were about forty people waiting in the out-patients, thirty-five of them with burns and in pain. Julian found the light very dazzling. He wanted a lemon, badly. His mouth was thick and dry. He wondered if his hearing had been affected as everything seemed very hushed and calm. Perhaps it was just the contrast. All the casualties were silent. The doctors and nurses were not very cheerful. There were no side benefits, so to speak; not even tea. Just the big, bleak room, with duckboards, for some reason, and some screens at the far end.

Julian saw a notice marking the toilets and slowly he rose to his feet. He stood for a minute, supporting himself by holding on to a steel pillar which had notices stuck on it, about the prices of prescriptions. He was stronger than he had expected. There was no pain below. His legs worked.

He walked past the toilets into a yard at the back. By a stroke of fortune some hospital official, maybe a doctor, was paying off a cab. Dawn had broken. It was light.

Julian took the cab. He brushed his coat and trousers as they travelled. He retied his tie to cover the tear in the yellow shirt. He thought "She tore that."

The policemen at the counter were helpful and polite. They had no reason to think that Julian had taken an active part in a riot which they preferred to call a students' disturbance: one senior had already publicly described it as "a stupid rag that got out of hand for a while".

Julian said who he was, he named his college and his title and was treated with respect. He explained that he had come north to a wedding in Lochearnhead and late in the evening had been visiting other friends in Ramsay Gardens. The policemen had no reason to disbelieve this polite, tired don.

When Julian made enquiries about the brave man who had gone to rescue the woman in the burning house the officer could give him no official information but reported that a body had been found. Julian said that he had met the man, but had not known his name. He had talked with him at the edge of the disturbance, also with a constable who was helpful to him.

Julian did not rush the act. He was given the name and the address of 101R. He left the police station.

The next cab took him to the new blocks of flats the other side of Buchanan Street station. 101R, whose name

was Michael Donald, lived in flat 42 in the block called
Sutherland House which had been built at that stage of
the 1950s when architects favoured bright colours. There
were slabs of green and black and red to brighten up the
concrete.

The staircase had green tiles and there had either been
tiles or metal strips at the edge of each concrete step; but
they had been torn away. Names were written on the
walls, but they were not clear because the finish was
rough, except where there were tiles: the architects had
thought of that.

The corridor of the fourth floor was quite wide and at
the end, at the angle of the building, an open area basked
in the morning sun. There was a washing-line which ran
from the two iron rings set in the concrete and for a
moment Julian thought that a towel, or maybe a sheet
had fallen off and was lying billowing on the floor. It lay
expiring by the concrete bannister or low wall, at the
building's edge. He had to walk that way, round this
strange open corner, to get to number 42.

It was not a sheet on the floor; nor a towel. It was a
child in convulsions. A boy of about four. Julian knelt by
him. It was not the first time he had had to cope with this
kind of fit and he took a small garment from the washing-
line. By the time he had rolled it up ready to put in the
child's mouth, the fit was over. The convulsions died
away. The child slowly came round.

A man passing by said "Oh, Danny, are you a'right
then, son?"

The boy blinked vaguely.

The man said "He's number 42," then passed on his
way.

Julian could not lift the boy, so he waited beside him and thought "Of course he'd have to be 42."

The boy came back to life. He stood up just as if he'd slipped and fallen for a second. He held out his hand. He led Julian home.

His father was not recognizable as a policeman. He wore very clean, inexpensive but well-chosen clothes. He had spiky hair and a bird-like face. His nice grey pullover showed that his hips were nearly as wide as his shoulders. He looked a little like a pear.

"Oh—dearie me," he said kindly. "I wondered where he'd got. You're very kind. His mother's out today. She's out at Cambuslang, and I must have nodded off. Come in, come in."

He disappeared for a moment to the kitchen. Everything in the flat was bright and nice and common and clean.

"What about our new carpet?" 101R asked as he came back. It was not yet properly laid. It was a brilliant orange colour. He said "It's the wife likes the bright colours. I must say, I've got used to them."

As he talked he gave his son a glass of water and a pill. Then the boy went into the bedroom and played with some toy.

101R said "It's not epilepsy, you know. We've had half the medicos in Scotland on Danny."

"Does he often—?"

"Not so bad, now. He's coming through. There was a point when we had twenty or thirty a day. But we're down in the single figures now. It's something you come to live with. The people hereabouts are good about it. And the other kids. I'm glad we don't live in Edinburgh. They're not the same over there."

Julian no longer remembered what he had intended to say or do to the policeman. He had wanted to reduce him, somehow, to call him out, to warn him "You take care, you brute." But that hadn't been possible. He'd seen both sides of the barricades.

He felt the pain as he came down those strange, cool, concrete stairs. By the time he reached the first storey he realized that he would collapse if he tried to go on.

He subsided. He sat on one of the steps and rested his shoulders and face against the cold tile. It was not the same crab. It did not seem like the same crab. The light kept fading. The spasms seemed to have a direct effect on his vision as if he were looking through a plate of glass which was filmed over now and then in a green kind of milk, a liquid not unlike that in the bottle in his pocket.

He did not recognize the crab. It was a strange, a very strange soft crab, not the old friend at all. It was a crab from the bottom of the snows.

He woke from an eternity and was surprised to do so. He thought I will walk again, just walk away from here. There were not so many people in the streets below. Women with big prams.

Long, long after, in the sunlight, a man helped him into a taxi and he remembered not the Kenilworth but the Central Hotel. In his mind, as they drove was a problem. That was all. Some kind of logical problem that would not be solved. An equation that came back again and again but would not work out; that beggared solution; that had a variable too many.

The porter said there was a message from his wife and handed him Mozart's note.

Chapter Thirteen

H E supposed for a moment, as he woke, that he was
dead. There was absolutely no point of reference in
the room. Light, ceiling, curtains, window, roof; all
strange. The roof outside was of lead. Then he felt the
pressure on his hand and turned and said "Love" vaguely,
as if he expected to find his mother.

It wasn't her. It wasn't Christabel.

He told Sally "Oh darling, I never thought to see you
again."

"I don't wonder," she said. "You are a bastard. You
might have come and tried to bail me out."

And he could tell she was playing the game. He was in
some hospital again.

She said "If it hadn't been for Mozart you would never
have. He found me. I was worried stiff where you must
have got. Last I saw of you, the bloody law was cracking
open your poor head."

The game. Her voice was too cheerful by half. Too
bright.

He said "I can't pee any more. Or the other thing."

"They'll fix that," she said. "Julian, I'm here." He

could see her fighting the tears. That's why she turned away.

"Look at this, though." She had a morning paper.

What morning?

On the front page of this paper there was a photograph of students in a road, or street.

She said "It's just close to the Kenilworth, there."

He found it hard to focus.

She helped him with a pillow.

He said "God damn." She wasn't good at shifting him.

She said "Come on, you've got to see this."

The photograph showed her being carried shoulder high and she was holding a plain flag.

"Red, of course," she said. "Turned out I was the only girl they put in the cooler. D'you suppose it'll be in the English edition? Just imagine what Mum'll say. Mind, Den usually gets the papers first. He'll hide it, I dare say."

Sally talked and talked; couldn't stop talking:

Hey, they asked me what I wanted. The journalists, I mean. There was three or four reporters when we come back by the Kenilworth. They asked me "Miss Cohen", had I anything to say. They said how come I'm risking life and limb in this cause and not a student or artist myself. They found out how I didn't have a boy there. Of course me, I don't know what to say. Except as show how hard the police had hit me and you and everybody. But I've been thinking ever since, really, why it was so wonderful. Whether it was just the excitement of you and me, it's been a time. But how you said "our side", how when we come over that barrier inside the square we knew, we *knew* we was the right side. How easy it is to risk every bloody thing. And I thought there must be some reason why it felt so natural that side: all one.

You've fallen asleep again, haven't you? Or have you just switched me off?

You're asleep.

I'm not going, Julian, not whatever anybody says.

I can't explain it to them. I'm not going to try. They say what *do* you want, if you burn things down, what will you put in their place? ... Some of the boys had answers for them, you know, about the syllabus or participation or individual rights and that. I can't tell them how I felt. I can't tell them how I seen your face in the middle of it. I can tell them how poor darling Matthew, who we didn't half understand, was one of us. And what it was like. And what it could be like, all like that. I don't know how the hell you knew that was for us.

Sleep.

They'll not take me away.

I'd still fancy Josh. I'd still love Josh. I would. But hey—

It's not the same. Nothing's the same when you've felt it like last night... how it could be. You gave me how it could be. I didn't understand before where you were at. Why you asked me all these endless questions about everything about me. I didn't know myself but now I felt it. It's as if all life's been half cock. And violent dreams in the middle of the night. They all come together, my darling, darling Julian. They all come together, I don't know why, don't know how, but they all happened together under the fire last night. I wish to Christ I could give you half my guts now, I feel so good.

Sally talked and talked:

The nurses were very good to her. They never asked who she was. They brought lots of coffee and she ate the meals he did not wake to eat.

It was a strange, spooky kind of nursing home. It was run by some Scottish nurses' association but the thing it lacked most was nurses. They came on and then went. The same nurse never seemed to come back again, and even the sisters were all on their way somewhere else.

Julian's room was quite big. There was space enough for three beds, but there was only one in it. The floor was polished linoleum. She knew she ought to go out and get some flowers.

"Hey, what about money, you better give me some money, or a cheque. I've quite run out. What do you do, anyway, do you just take a cheque to any bank and say 'I'm Miss Cohen, pay up'? How long d'you have to wait? Julian? Julian?"

With his eyes still closed he said "If you look in my coat pocket you'll find a cheque book."

"You're crafty, aren't you? How am I supposed to know when you're awake?"

"I'm always awake."

"I expect you are. Except you switch me off."

"I don't."

"D'you mind me talking?"

"No."

"I'll look in your coat."

"I haven't peed yet, have I?"

"Not yet."

"How long—?"

"Which pocket? Inside one?" She found it and said "Whoopee, I got you where I want you now. How much are you going to give me?"

She wasn't good at shifting him.

"Tell you what, I'll call the nurse."

"No."

"We're paying, aren't we?"

"Just push the . . . push that pillow, I . . ."

"Look, I'll ring the nurse."

"No."

The writing on the cheque was all over the place, even though it was three hours after an injection.

He made it out for a million pounds, and laughing she began to cry and put her head on the bed.

"Leave it there."

"What, like this?"

"Stay."

"Darling, I can't stay all the time like this, I'll rick my neck."

"Stay."

Ten minutes later, she was in pain, but she was still in exactly the same position, pitched forward with her head on the bed and his fingers clutched in her hair. The cheque was smudged where it lay beneath her cheek.

"Don't go, darling. Live," said both.

He said "Christabel?"

Sally stayed absolutely still.

Oh look down, God. Is there never an end to your twists?

Chapter Fourteen

THE medical profession don't care for attempted
suicides. They weren't therefore too kind to Christabel. She was taken to a hospital in a district called
Barlinnie, which is more famous for its gaol.

"A sister organization, I presume," Christabel said,
when Mozart told her that.

He came to take her away. He told her where Julian
was: where, more or less, he had been.

She said "I wonder what the Glasgow Hospital Board
would do without us?" as they drove out through the
gate.

They stopped for coffee in the Mozart pad. He'd told
her most of the tale.

Christabel asked, apparently by the way, "What kind
of sports do these lunatics at the Allan Ramsay play?"

"Not much."

"You said you went up there?"

Mozart sounded tired. He said "I thought they might
like to learn lacrosse. I had these sticks."

She laughed. She said "That greatly reassures me. I
must say, they're not my favourite people. If they stuck to

their manifesto, I might be with them, but really, what do they expect to gain by burning the place to the ground? I saw that picture in the paper, by the way. Where is our little Sally now?" She wished she'd just said "Sally".

Mozart dodged it, to begin with.

He said "What's 'peek-a-boo'?"

"Ah."

He said "When you were on the bed you said something that sounded like 'peek-a-boo'."

"That's because it was 'peek-a-boo' I said."

"So?"

"You surprise me. You haven't read the texts. Nine out of ten suicides are futile murders, or so they say. The victim simply doesn't have the guts to kill somebody else so he or she turns the knife inwards, instead. But the tenth case is even more futile and feeble than the others. He or she is simply playing charades. Only when the poison has been swallowed does the idiot concerned have a sudden, sinking realization that he or she will not actually be there to witness the post mortem scene. Hence Peek-a-boo, a childish game . . . For the last two days in Barlinnie's second gaol, I have been trying to persuade myself that the sight of that little bitch's lock of hair made me fit to murder her. But I am forced to the conclusion that my first instinctive analysis, made on that bed, was the correct one. In spite of my nice manners, I don't like being up-staged. I am therefore that most despicable of characters, the failed peek-a-boo . . . I asked you where she was?"

They were drinking champagne, for the sake of unborn referees. Mozart looked unhappy about the recurring question.

Christabel said in one breath "She's there with him in the hospital, don't tell me, how vulgar. How the hell did she find out where he was?"

"Oh shit," Mozart said. "Does it matter?"

"Not really. But how did she? He'd left her. He'd walked out, he stayed with me hours after they gave me that awful stomach pump. He collapsed, damn it, by my bed in Barlinnie. He got moved to the nursing home, I see that. But how did she get back to him?"

"He'd told me where she was."

"Oh no—" Christabel said.

"She'd be bound to find out—"

"Oh, Mozart, I thought you were supposed to be on my side."

He looked horribly guilty. And then rather angry. "Frankly," he said "I didn't ask to get involved in all this in the first place."

"Yes, you did."

"I didn't."

"Mozart, I'm not at all sure that you don't yourself play some pretty tricky games."

He had a cigarette: an unheard-of cigarette.

He said "Christ Almighty this is one of the situations in life that suddenly makes you into a guilty schoolboy all over again."

"Because you've been indiscreet."

"It's the couple."

"Mozart."

"It's the couple. Someone gives you all their confidences. Then another person gives you all their confidences."

"You can tell them not to."

"I knew you'd be angry."

"Well I am. I am . . . I am. The name for someone who takes in everybody's confidences, by the way, is a gossip. You're a gossip."

"I'm not malevolent. Steady on."

"You're certainly not my friend if you gave that girl his nursing home address."

"I did."

"Tut . . . Did he ask for her?"

"No he didn't."

"You promise? That's vital to me."

"I promise."

She gathered her things together: her coat and bag.

He said "Christabel, I'm sorry, but don't let's let a perfectly understandable everyday stupid kind of indiscretion like that spoil what was obviously growing up between you and me. I mean she's not the same kind of—"

"Don't say any more. It is no good denying what exists when it exists." She looked back at him over her shoulder as she started down the little narrow stairs. She said "A cool exists. I don't know if it always will, nor do you. But I think you betrayed me a little. Therefore a cool exists."

"Shall I run you—"

"No thank you."

"Please."

"All right. If you wish."

In the car he said "Look, she's just got a pretty face, but she has got a pretty face."

Christabel didn't reply to that.

Chapter Fifteen

CHRISTABEL said "I honestly don't think you should fall asleep on the bed like that," and Sally woke with a start. The cheque for a million pounds was still sticking to her cheek.

Sally said meekly "He wants me here."

Christabel had brought flowers, champagne, some magazines and eau-de-cologne. Also a sponge-bag with a whole set of new wash-things and three different types of soap.

She said "It's far too hot in here," and opened the window. Then she went and stood over by the bed and smiled down at Julian.

"Darling, you're all right?" he asked.

"Quite all right," Christabel replied, and chuckled as she added "Re-enter Peek-a-boo."

Sally didn't move.

If Julian was confused by the presence of the two girls, he certainly disguised his discomfort very well. He said "I hear everything, you know. Bloody doctors always say things to the nurses over your face as if you were already buried but—"

"You're not going to die," Sally said. And it was awful. She had somehow struck completely the wrong note.

Julian paused a moment and then went on talking to Christabel. He said "You'd think they'd ascertain the effects of the drugs they prescribe but they're such bloody inaccurate butchers, all of them."

"Stop puffing and blowing, darling. What is it you want?" Christabel asked.

"Cheque," he said vaguely.

Sally had folded up the cheque for the million. He turned to her a little irritably and waved his hand; fluttered it, from the wrist.

"The cheque book."

"Oh," Sally said. She stood up. It had dropped on the floor. When she bent down her pants showed. Christabel observed them. Julian apparently, for once, did not.

Sally said "Here we are," in the wrong voice again. In her mother's voice, when her mother visited the sick. She said "And the pen," and put them on the bed.

Julian wanted support to sit up. Sally still had not learnt to shift him, and she herself was getting very tired.

She said "I been up three nights running."

And Christabel said flatly, quickly, "Poor little you."

Christabel knew how to shift him, in the bed. She knew how to angle the pillows. She knew he needed the bed tray to support the cheque book.

He nodded his thanks.

He said to Sally "How much for? Fifty?"

Christabel said "Aren't you going to give her more than that?"

He said "Leave it, Christabel."

Sally said "I don't know, darling. I just haven't got anything."

He wrote out a cheque for a hundred pounds.

"No, I don't need all that," Sally said.

He said "Look in my coat."

"There's a fiver there. I saw," Sally said.

"Take it."

"But I don't need anything now."

"Take it."

"I'm not planning on going anywhere," Sally said.

"Love," he held out his hand. She took it.

She said "All right. I'll come back at ten. I'll come back to say good night. I could do with some sleep. I'll come back at ten, all right?"

She glanced at Christabel as she named the hour the second time.

"I've got the message," Christabel said, and giggled. "Christ." She turned back to the window and lit a cigarette. Julian closed his eyes. Sally went to the wardrobe and put his cheque book back in his coat pocket. She took a fiver, the cheque for a hundred, the cheque for a million and also an unmarked plain envelope from his wallet: a most important envelope.

Christabel was telling Julian "You should count yourself lucky. You should have seen the ward they put me in after you left . . ."

Christabel said "I rang home, there are two letters from the boys. And I rang the school. They're all right. The College has been after you for some reason. I think they probably need some signature on that B.U.P.A. stuff. Oh God, I'm so glad I didn't . . . Julian? Julian . . . What got into me I can't think. What an odd city this is."

Julian had closed his eyes. He began to moan and cry and turn.

Christabel rang for a nurse who was a long time in coming.

She said "I think we might have another injection, nurse."

"It's not time yet."

"I still think—"

"I've got my orders."

"Then ask Sister to come along."

Christabel stepped out of the room to talk to the Sister, who refused to change the doctor's instructions concerning the quantities of drugs.

Christabel asked the Sister to ring the doctor. The Sister said she did not know where the doctor might be. Christabel told the Sister to find another doctor.

The Sister said "There's only the Registrar."

"Then get the Registrar."

"He'll be round at seven."

"Get him for me now, please, Sister."

The Sister did not look pleased.

She came back to say that the Registrar would be pleased to speak to Miss Cohen on the phone.

Christabel made her identity plain to both the Sister, and then on the phone to the Registrar.

The Registrar talked to the Sister.

The Sister called the nurse.

Christabel returned to the room where Julian was now writhing and crying with pain.

Christabel put a hand over his and said "It's all right, my love. She's coming now. I've fixed it. She's on her way."

Julian said "Tell her to fucking hurry."

"She's coming."

The nurse arrived and administered the injection. She noted the time and the quantity in the book.

She said to Christabel "I can't help it, I have to do—"

"It's all right, nurse. I'm not blaming you."

"These bloody doctors," Julian said.

"Hush," Christabel told him.

He sighed. She put a hand on his again and feebly he gripped her thumb.

"Sleep," Christabel told him.

"I haven't peed yet, have I?"

"Sleep, my love."

He never regained consciousness.

But he lived on. Lord, how we hang on, if we aren't so very old. For the wives that's the worst of it.

At ten o'clock the specialist and doctor were both in the room with Christabel when Sally walked in. They were talking in low voices.

Talking over the bed, talking right in front of him, as if he were dead, Sally thought. And they were saying terrible things, discussing how long he had to go. They said with an ordinary kidney case it would be possible to operate, to put in an artificial irrigation plant which might relieve the poison and the strain on the heart. As they talked, Julian moved, quite violently, with a little "huh" noise, his whole body flipping like a fish on a rock. Instinctively Sally moved forward to him and said "It's me, Sally." She said it very quietly.

But the specialist heard her. He broke off what he was

saying to Christabel to tell her "He's not conscious I'm afraid, that's just the effect of the uric acid which is infiltrating through his whole system."

Sally was made to feel stupid. She was almost frightened to take Julian's hand. She wanted to kiss the back of it. She felt embarrassed to do so. Like a child who has been told not to be silly she waited until the others had turned their backs then quickly bent down and kissed his brow. Blushing, she sat down on the same chair, an ordinary wooden upright chair, close by the bed.

The specialist said "In this case, you understand . . ."

"Too well," Christabel said. "But he will be kept under, now?"

"Of course."

"There was some question, earlier this evening."

The specialist apologized. He would see that an order was given that any amount of pain-killing drugs could be used now. "Without restriction," he said, flatly.

Christabel said "I suppose it's just a matter of how long the heart can stand it now."

"It's still quite strong."

"I see."

Sally spoke up. She said "Then why don't you operate?"

The specialist looked right through her. He treated her as if she were a child, or possibly a housemaid. The party moved out into the corridor.

Sally felt tears of rage form in her eyes. She thought, they haven't the nerve to keep me out forcibly, they might make me a member of the wedding now. She wondered who the specialist thought she was: whether he guessed right; whether Julian had told him.

Julian sighed and jumped again.

She whispered to him "I'm here. I said I'd be back. I'm not going to leave, not what any of them say or don't say." She wanted to tell him she was scared. His eyes were closed. The lids looked swollen. His face was white like marble and his brow was glowing with sweat. His breathing was coming much shorter. She noticed the difference. She said "They've filled you up with drugs, I expect." She found the little pad of eau-de-cologne which Christabel had prepared and she thought "Why didn't he tell me? I could have made one of those." She dabbed his brow.

Then Christabel came back into the room. The lights were all off except the blue one by the door. It took her a moment to get used to the dimness. She stood smoking, then moved round to the other side of the bed.

Sally thought, I know what she's saying to herself. She's saying "That little girl is behaving in the worst of taste," I know that's what she's thinking. But that's not going to budge me now.

Christabel finished a glass of champagne she had left on the window sill. She said "D'you want some? There's a bit left in the bottle."

"All right," Sally said.

Christabel found another toothmug. Maybe one day hospitals will get round to catering for the dying and leave ice and good glasses and proper ashtrays for the patients' relations. Meantime, everyone has to play the hospital game. They use saucers for ashtrays, toothmugs for champagne.

Sally took a drink. She never left his side. She thought to herself "The way I sit like this and she moves about so easily makes me the loser here, I see that, but I can't get myself to leave his side." She stretched forward when he muttered something. She took his hand. He gripped hers quite tightly and wouldn't let her go. She thought, That's right then, you hang on to me. She thought, God make it a miracle now. Take Matthew's death in exchange. She thought, make it a marvellous miracle through my wrist and hand.

Christabel said "That jumping's horrid isn't it?"

Sally admitted "Yes."

After an hour or two, when he was muttering and sighing more frequently, Christabel said "I think I'd better ring nurse. It's three hours since he had his last jab. He's having horrid dreams."

Sally didn't know what to say. She just sat still until the nurse came in and moved her a little in order to give the injection. When the nurse went out again she said "He's breathing longer again."

Christabel said "He will for a while."

Sally said "You've had a lot of experience of illness. I can see that."

"Only with Julian," Christabel said, "and his children."

Sally said "I know you may think this sounds sly, but if you want to go, I promise, I'll make a pact, I'll ring if—"

"You don't need to. I'm going at three. I've arranged with Sister that she should call me."

"You're at the Central, or with Mozart?"

"At the Central. I gather you got on well with Mozart?"

"He didn't like me at first, not a bit."

Julian cried and his whole body jumped and snatched. Did it again and again.

"Hey," Christabel said, fixing his pillows. "Stop leaping about the place, old man."

Sally said "I promise I'd ring, anyway." She thought to herself, I wonder why I say that. Christabel was gathering together her things. She came to the end of the bed and squeezed Julian's toe through the blankets. Then she swept out of the room.

"She's got more style than I thought," Sally admitted to herself.

His breathing was short and now it had grown horribly irregular. Sometimes there would be a long, long pause before he inhaled again. To begin with, Sally tried to will him through these pauses—"Come on, come on, breathe in." It wasn't that he was exactly in pain. But it seemed to be an awful nightmare, going on and on. He kept muttering, but nothing she could make out. He still held her hand.

She thought "I should ring Christabel", and not very long after, when the breathing grew even more peculiar, she thought "Maybe I'd better do so now." Then: "No, it's in my mind. He's just the same."

She thought, Christabel has cool, leaving me like this. I don't think I'd have done that. But he's really mine. I don't suppose he knows I'm here. I would ring Christabel, mind. I don't want to cheat her.

Then into her mind slipped the thought, I'd really prefer that she was here. I don't honestly want to be alone. I've never been with someone dead, not in a room. I suppose with Julian it would be different.

Then it occurred to her. It would be worse with him. With Julian dead.

Yet by dawn, there was a funny contradiction. She was scared he would die, but it wasn't when he paused and didn't inhale for as many as twenty seconds that she felt fear. It was when he breathed in again, suddenly noisily. His throat rattled and she thought that must be the death rattle but then it kept happening all the time.

The nurse came in with some tea and she was glad of that. A doctor came in and checked the heart beat.

Sally asked "How long?" And she knew the situation had turned over. She was really asking "How much longer do I have to wait?" She was beginning to push him over and she felt bad and panicky and bewildered by that. She took his hand again and prayed and said "God give us a miracle. I don't want him to die. I want him to be well. I don't want him to be like this."

He seemed to be struggling to breathe.

Then at six-thirty in the morning Christabel came back in. She looked fresh. She hadn't slept but had bathed and she smelt very feminine and clean.

Sally felt herself to be clammy and dirty as if she had been two nights in a train. She smiled at Christabel. She said when the last injection had been. She spoke about the breathing.

Christabel said "You'd better take a walk around. The garden's quite nice."

"No."

"It could go on for another day."

"How do you know? Could it?"

"The doctor said so when I rang."

She was in touch with the doctors, they told her things.

Sally thought, It's just a piece of paper, isn't it, a marriage, but she's counted all the way, I don't even get half a vote. When I've a daughter, I'll see she never goes ten feet near a married man.

"You see the window from the garden," Christabel said. "If anything happened, I'd wave."

"Okay."

They were with him, together, when the end came. Two or three times, he stopped breathing for so long that they thought it was over and almost rose from their places each side of the bed. Then suddenly he shuddered and breathed and that awful muscular contraction happened again. They both had an arm over his body to try and quieten the painful jerks. It was as if he had hiccoughs of the spine. He groaned and whimpered. Sally hardly dared look at him, but held onto his right hand, and occasionally put her cheek down against his fingers.

Then she sat up and saw that Christabel was in exactly the same position the other side. She also was exhausted.

Sally turned her eyes to Julian's face. He was bolstered with pillows and his head had fallen forward.

She said "His lips." They had begun to lose their colour.

Again, so faintly he breathed again.

"He's still alive," Christabel said and as she spoke he must have died.

The thought that occurred to both women simultaneously was "Thank God he's gone."

The Sister came in and made sure, then she and Christabel changed the pillows so he lay back. He looked a little oriental, in death. Sally cried. She couldn't stop the tears.

Christabel also cried, and they finished the last dregs of the champagne when the Sister left the room.

"I'll go first," Sally said.

"Yes, you will," Christabel replied. It was an unnecessary thing to say. Her only bad move.

Sally went at once. She hardly glanced at the body on the bed. She said "Bye-bye," either to Christabel or him.

Christabel walked over to the bed, thought what a foul, foul, foul disease it is, and covered his beautiful face with the sheet. She thought "I dread telling the boys."

Chapter Sixteen

IT was one of those towns which the Tudors seemed to have built purposely and malevolently in order to depress twentieth-century private schoolboys. There were tea-shops and tuck-shops, a market place without a market and a Trust House hotel.

As Christabel came out of the school gates she was thinking several thoughts at once, in the way we do, for weeks after a crisis. She was thinking, Gosh, I suppose I'll have to sell this car. What an awful little coward I am. It's much better to do it this way, I mean leave it until the holidays. Why is that man hooting at me? What an awful proper gloomy show-piece of a town this is. I haven't got my indicator out. I suppose it is idiotic of me staying in that house. I don't really want to go back there. That man looks like Mozart. Yet I wouldn't give the house up for anything. Stop hooting at me. The boys need every bit of security they can get. That is Mozart. Lord. As Julian would say: Lord. I don't want to talk to Mozart. Mozart is the sort of Glaswegian who is absolutely lovely in Glasgow. How peculiar he looks. Perhaps that's because he's out of a track suit.

"Mozart, what on earth are you doing here?"

"I'm chasing you."

"How super to see you."

"They told me on the phone. I rang your home." He said "A girl told me you were up to see the boys. I thought you might need moral support."

She said "I do, really," and began to giggle.

He said "Where are the boys then?"

"Last time I saw them they were in the junior school garden eating some measly strawberries from a single plate. Isn't that awful?"

Mozart said "I'm not quite tuned in. You mean you're not bringing them out?"

"No, I'm not."

"The girl said—"

"I was going to. But I saw them from a distance and they looked so sweet and timid and sad already I just ran the other way. Nobody's seen me. I didn't tell anybody I was coming."

Mozart shook his head. "These bloody prep schools. Why do you do it?"

"Why?" she agreed.

"Shall we have tea here?"

"No."

"D'you know somewhere?"

"Follow me."

She drove, as always, far too fast.

It was more of a café, really; behind some petrol pumps. Mozart said "Does the news surprise you?"

She thought and smoked and answered "It doesn't move me, if that's what you mean."

"That's not what I mean."

"It's the privilege of those of us who survive violent acts of self-destruction to despise others who do the same thing, even if they make a success of it. Have you been to Half Moon Lane?"

"Yes. I met her step-father there. He's very nice. He's called Den. He said 'Hello Mr Anderson, I'm Den.' He was clearing up her things. There was no sign of anyone else. Evidently the other girl friend left, after the weekend of the holocaust. Den seemed to know very little about all that. He said that he thought the cause was over an American boy because he had sent back all her love letters without comment. She was evidently engaged to him. Den thought she died of a broken heart. He said he was doing his best to stop her mother Pam writing a bad letter to this poor man. I said I thought he'd better do that."

"How did she do it?"

"Very sadly, really. And kind of efficiently. It was gas from the stove in the kitchen at the back. She'd been out with the boys in her digs, then they went off for the weekend and she stayed back. She went to her bank on the Saturday morning and put in sixty pounds. She wrote this letter to me saying how she wanted the money to go to Julian's boys. She bought half a bottle of vodka and some lemons. I went up to that little shop where she got all her stores and they said she was her usual self, talking about going to California. They thought she was a wee bit disappointed in Glasgow because she didn't win the swimming. They were pleased to hear that one of the girls in her race has since been disqualified because she never paid her entrance fee. A medal for coming third therefore goes to Sally's mother. They like her very much in the shops . . . She drank all the vodka before she fell asleep, also the pills, maybe pinched from Julian. There was a plain envelope. Nobody found her before I got the letter on Monday morning and I rang the police and this Bell and Croyden where Den works. It all went according to her plan."

"I suppose it's a text-book case. The blow she didn't dare to aim at me."

"You never know, do you? There are so many reasons, always. That seems to me the only truth. There's even social factors, isn't there?"

"I don't think I was any bloodier than I might be expected to be." Christabel seemed tougher, which is to say, less inclined to talk. "Mozart, are you going north again?"

"Yes."

"Why don't you stop off the night with me?"

"I was thinking about that."

"Good."

"I said I was. I lied to you. I didn't go into your house but I looked at it, then I went along to your village post office and rang." He seemed to find it hard to explain his difficulties. He said at last, with a sad grin "It's the pony in the paddock, isn't it?"

She burst out laughing, and nodded, and said "How right you are."

"I mean, even if your friends went out of their way to be nice. It's the pony in the paddock."

She said "D'you remember when I told you in your room that my heart was broken?"

"I'll never forget."

"I think it's a good thing that it had bust. Otherwise I

never would have coped. Now I can synthesize. I can impose a pattern more or less the same shape as the design that was emerging until the cancer came. That means the pony in the paddock," she admitted, stubbing out her cigarette.

"And the two wee boys apart there, eating off the single plate?"

"They'll come through. That's the point of these schools. I'm not going to weaken there."

Mozart accepted it.

Only on his way north did he think of all the things he should have said to her; how she was doing for her children what she had done for Julian, how she was turning her eyes from the blazing truth that passions such as Julian's have always deeper roots? How we can't go on and on, like this?

Nor can we keep under-paying Association football referees in this ridiculous way, he thought. That's a damned outrage. That really is.